MERLIN KILLS A ZOMBIE

MOLLY FITZ

Whiskered Mysteries
PO Box 72
Brighton, MI 48116

ABOUT THIS BOOK

When my cat brought me a dead bird as a present, I cringed.

When that dead bird suddenly flitted back to life, I screamed.

At first, I shrugged it off as one of the random things that happens when your roommate is a magical cat, but then it kept happening.

Turns out a familiar foe is creating an army of undead creatures with the goal of forcing us to surrender. But Merlin and I refuse to let dark magic prevail—not when the entire existence of magic is now at stake.

And if magic dies, so too will all who wield it.

Oh no, my cat will NOT become a casualty in this unholy war. I'm ready to fight my way through a million zombies and then take out the big bad, too. Nothing can come between this witchy cat and his familiar—and I'm ready to prove it.

AUTHOR'S NOTE

Hey, new reader friend!

Welcome to the crazy inner workings of my brain. I hope you'll find it a fun and exciting place to be.

If you love snarky talking animals and crazy magical mishaps as much as I do, then I'm pretty sure you're going to enjoy the journey ahead.

This book is just one of my many brain-tickling adventures to come, so make sure you keep in touch to keep in the know!

I've done my best to make it easy by offering several fun ways to access sneak peeks of upcoming books, monthly giveaways, adorable pictures of my own personal feline overlords, and many other cool things that are just for my inner circle of readers.

So take a quick moment now to choose your favorite:

Download my app
Join my VIP reader group
Sign up for my newsletter
Kick off a cat chat on Facebook

Okay, ready to talk to some animals and solve some mysteries?

Let's do this!
    Molly Fitz

WHOA. DID I MISS SOMETHING?

This story references some events that you haven't had the chance to read about yet. Worry not! You'll be able to read about Merlin and Luna's beautiful cat-witch wedding in LUNA THE MAGICKLESS FLUFF, coming this fall as part of a special cozy mystery anthology.

And believe me...

If you've never been to a magical cat wedding, then you are definitely missing out! But with so many supernatural creatures gathered in one small space, there's bound to be a kerfuffle or two. Luckily, Gracie Springs, resident human, wedding planner, and familiar extraordinaire, is on the case.

Subscribe to Molly's newsletter so you don't miss this special bonus story set in the world of MERLIN THE MAGICAL FLUFF!

You can do that here: MollyMysteries.com/subscribe

*H*ey there, I'm Gracie Springs. I'm a twenty-something barista working my way through grad school. Okay, I should have gotten my degree several months ago, but I haven't found the time to finish my thesis yet.

You can't really blame me, all things considered. Seriously, you try working as the human familiar for a magical cat with at least two dangerous enemies and tell me how well you keep up with the everyday things.

Ever since my Maine Coon Merlin revealed his powers to me, it's been one attempt on my life after another.

When I first moved to the tiny Georgia

town of Elderberry Heights, it was just me and my normal kitty cat living in the house my grandmother gifted me when she retired to the Florida Keys. But now Merlin's pregnant wife Luna has joined us, and so has Luna's former familiar, a somewhat disgruntled and super evil ghost named Virginia.

Yeah, it's getting a little cramped, and the kittens haven't even been born yet!

Another fun twist?

I'm descended from King Arthur, and my witchy cat has a famous lineage, too. He's descended from the original Merlin.

No, not the human imposter everyone thinks they know. The real wizard, who just so happened to be a cat.

Because of our intertwined ancestry, Merlin and I have a nearly unbreakable bond. It's also put a gigantic target on both of our backs.

Our original enemy, Dash, hasn't turned up for a while, but we have no doubt she's regrouping and will make a play for us again soon.

What she wants with us, I honestly have no idea. And I'm almost too afraid to find out.

Because honestly? The more I learn about

the magical world, the less I seem to under-stand it. I can't cast magic, but I can hold it inside of me. That's my main role as Merlin's familiar, in fact: to be a walking vessel for his magical overflow. If he were a normal witch, becoming tied to him wouldn't have upset my life all that much.

However, since my cat is anything but normal, it's one life-or-death encounter after the next.

It may seem like I'm complaining, but actually I'm happy to help. Someone has to take on the bad guys, after all.

So why not me?

Famous last words, I know...

"*E*ek! Why me?" I shrieked when Merlin dropped a dead bird at my feet just as I was trying to fix my morning coffee.

"It's a gift," the fluffy Maine Coon announced with pride. He didn't even seem the least bit offended by my reaction to his grotesque gesture.

I cringed as I studied the limp avian form at

my feet. "What could possibly make you think I'd want this?"

"Why wouldn't you want this?" he countered. The tip of his tail flicked, revealing the beginnings of his irritation with me. "And how can you know you don't like it until you try it?"

Proof that even though we could talk to each other, we didn't necessarily stand one another.

"Um, thank you," I said, bending down to examine the "gift" more closely. I'd have to find some way to dispose of it when he wasn't looking. The problem was, Merlin always seemed to be looking.

"See, now that wasn't so hard," my cat said, a smug smile spreading across his whiskered face.

I was trying to work out what to say next—it took quite a bit longer when I hadn't yet had my coffee for the day—when the bird flitted to life.

I screamed and fell backward, landing hard on my butt.

"Don't worry, Gracie!" Merlin cried as he pounced into action. "I'll save you from this feathered fiend!"

I watched in stunned silence as he leapt into the air, sunk his fangs into the bird, then landed back on the linoleum floor, all in one fluid motion.

"Coulda... sworn—he's... dead," he mumbled through a mouthful of bird. Then much to my horror, he crunched down hard.

Oh, that poor little red-breasted robin.

Merlin dropped the now thoroughly murdered bird at my feet again, then began to groom himself with long, sweeping licks across his side.

I didn't know what to say. I certainly couldn't force out another thank you, but I also couldn't really punish my cat for doing exactly what cats do.

As I stared at the bird in bewilderment, it began to twitch back to life. First it was just the tips of one wing, but then one black beady eye shot open.

I crab-walked backward until I bumped into the fridge.

"Oh no, you don't!" Merlin cried and pounced again before his victim could take flight.

He crunched down on it once more, this

time breaking its neck so that it hung at an
unnatural angle.

I breathed in and out deeply, praying that
such a scene would never ever unfold in my
kitchen again. Coffee or not, I was now fully
awake—and also undoubtedly scarred for life.

"Is it really dead now?" I whispered after a
brief pause, afraid that if I wasn't quiet enough,
my words would rouse the songbird from its
sleep of death. Provided it was actually dead
this time.

Merlin and I both stared down at the disfig-
ured mound of feathers and watched as it once
more twitched to life.

This was most assuredly not how I'd
planned to start the morning!

2

"*W*hy won't it die?" I cried, scrabbling for purchase as I attempted to push myself into a standing position.

"Dark magic is afoot," Merlin declared before pouncing on the dead-or-dying-or-undead bird. "Go to Luna. I'll take care of this fiend!"

Well, he didn't have to tell me twice. I ran out of the kitchen and straight through the front door without even taking the time to slip on a pair of shoes. The morning dew clung to my socks, but I didn't care. I could easily put on fresh footwear, but I couldn't stand to watch as

Merlin had his way with the sharp-beaked monster in the kitchen.

I rounded the house in a flash and found Luna sprawled out on the grass and soaking up the sun. Ever since becoming pregnant, she'd taken to spending much of her day in the back garden. I'd even helped her plant some flowers and herbs to help with the homesickness she sometimes felt.

Seeing me, she gently rolled onto her feet, still the perfect picture of grace and elegance even toward the end of her pregnancy.

Yes, we were getting quite close to kitten time. The cats had given me one week to plan their wedding after they'd found out they were expecting. They reasoned that since holy matrimony was important to humans and not so much to cats, I should be the one to put in all the work. That had been a few weeks ago now. The happy newlyweds had spent a couple of nights away from home to celebrate their honeymoon, and then life had gotten back to normal—well, as normal as it could be when you had two talking cats and a ghost as your roommates.

I'd almost started to believe that the

magical baddies of the world were done with us, but now we had a very messed-up robin to prove otherwise.

"Oh, dear," Luna said after noting my worn expression. "I told Merlin you wouldn't appreciate that gift, but he insisted. He said you hadn't been yourself since Virginia moved in, and he wanted to do something to show you that you're appreciated."

"That's actually kind of sweet," I said with a half smile as I rubbed at my sore backside. "But, yeah, you were right, the bird was a terrible idea. Especially considering it won't stay dead."

Luna's ears shot back, and her blue eyes grew wide. "What do you mean it won't stay dead?" she asked in a low whisper.

"Exactly that. That thing would seem dead, but then pop back up a few moments later. I'm pretty sure I watched Merlin break its neck, but even that didn't stop it." I shuddered at the memory—that one would, no doubt, reappear in my nightmares many times over. "Also I think maybe I'm a vegetarian now."

Luna hissed. "Don't even joke about such terrible things."

"Which of those things do you think was a joke?" I sputtered in disbelief.

Luna studied me for a moment. "Oh my, you are serious. Aren't you?"

"Dead serious," I said through gritted series. "Or, I guess, undead serious."

"Yes, that seems to be the situation we have on our hands now," Luna agreed with a solemn nod.

"Do you mean...?" I couldn't even finish the sentence. The very word seemed so improbable.

"Zombies," Luna confirmed my suspicion.

"But how?" I exploded, cursing our bad luck. Although something told me a lack of luck had nothing to do with this.

"The how is quite simple," Luna explained patiently. "It's the why I'm more worried about."

"Well, now you have me curious."

The she-cat stared at the house without saying anything.

"How are zombies made, Luna?" I prompted.

She blinked up into the sun, then turned to

me slowly. "Well, you know how cats have nine lives?"

"Sure," I said to hurry us along. I'd always assumed that was just an expression, but obviously not. I'd have to remember to ask about that later, when we weren't facing down a zombie in the kitchen.

"It's not all cats. Just witches. We're not immortal, but we are granted extra lives."

"Okay," I said, nodding. "I guess that makes sense."

"We can bestow our lives upon others. It's a complex but relatively well-known spell. Normally it's a benevolent spell used to help mates match each other's lifespans."

"But I'm guessing that's not the case with the bird Merlin brought me," I ventured.

"No," she said, searching the distance. "There's a corrupted version of the life-share spell. It can be used to reanimate the dead."

"But that bird only just died. I saw it," I reminded her.

Luna's face took on a drawn expression, which did not provide me with very much comfort. "Yes, that means our dark witch is close."

"Do you think he'll make more zombies?"

"I'm guessing the first one wasn't an accident, so more will likely be on the way."

"But why would someone surrender all their lives just to spook us a little?" That was the part I didn't understand. Even if we couldn't kill the bird, we were still much bigger and stronger and could find another way to overpower it.

"That's what worries most," Luna whispered. "The truly evil among us—the kind who would use a spell like this—can also control the minds and wills of others. It's possible the culprit has an army of helpless witches at his disposal and that each of them have a cadre of zombies at theirs."

I sighed and dragged a hand through my hair. "So things are about to get bad, huh?"

"Really bad," Luna bit out, as if speaking the words would also make them true.

Luna was the bravest among us. If this new zombie situation spooked her, then we were in for some tough times ahead.

This day just kept on getting worse and worse...

3

"Now that you know what we're dealing with here, I'm sure you understand that we can't leave Merlin alone with that thing any longer." Luna ran around the side of the house, back to the front.

I loped after her somewhat hesitantly. One undead songbird couldn't do that much on its own, but what about a whole flock of them? There's a reason Hitchcock's aptly titled masterpiece was one of the most enduring horror films of all time.

When I entered the house, I found Luna pacing tight, worried circles around Merlin, inspecting him closely. "Are you sure it didn't get a scratch or two in?"

Merlin puffed up his fur and then shook out his coat. "Even if it did, I'm fine. The life-share spell can't be conducted through a third party. If someone wants to turn me into a zombie, they'll have to do it face-to-face."

Luna let out a sad mewl. "That's what I'm worried about, dear."

Merlin rubbed his face against his wife's. "Don't worry about me, my love. Just keep growing our children in your belly, and I'll handle the rest."

Luna narrowed her eyes and flicked her tail. She loved Merlin, but she definitely didn't like being ousted from our adventures. When she'd still had her magic, she'd been the more powerful of the two cat-witches, and every now and then she seemed to question the sacrifice she'd made—whether that was fighting ghosts or inspecting strange noises at night.

"Luna caught me up on the magical side of things," I said with a nod her way. "I think I understand all that, but what happened to the bird?" I glanced around but didn't see the cursed thing.

Merlin strode across the kitchen and sat at my feet. "I defeated the vile fiend in the best, most enjoyable way possible." He paused, lifting his nose with obvious pride.

"You a—"

"I ate it!" Merlin finished with wide eyes. "I'm not usually a fan of dark magic meat, but a meal is a meal. And I had to get rid of it somehow. At least this way we know he won't be coming back."

I shuddered at the thought of the mangled carcass stirring in my cat's stomach. *Yuck, yuck, yuck.*

"But who would send a zombie after us, and why?" Luna asked, concern reflecting in her wide blue eyes.

"Surely you've noticed we collect enemies like they're going out of fashion," Merlin teased. "Granted, things have been suspiciously quiet for the last few weeks."

"Hang on. There's someone else we should be asking these questions," I murmured, then marched up and down the hallway, banging on the walls. "I know you're in there!" I shouted. "Come out. We need to talk to you!"

It didn't take long for one very angry ghost to phase through the wall and regard me with an icy glare.

If looks could kill... Actually I think our resident ghost was hoping her sour expression *would* render me dead, but she was completely powerless and also bound to our house.

Virginia spent most of her time inside the walls, the only real place she could get any privacy. At first she'd enjoyed popping in and out of rooms and trying to spook us, but the less we reacted to her jump-scares, the more she'd voluntarily begun to fade into the background.

Still, the former evil henchwoman might know something about our new zombie master foe. And anyway, it never hurt to check.

"Why did a zombie attack us today?" I demanded as she bobbed before me, nearly translucent from her lack of magical energy.

"Is that what all the fuss was about?" she asked drolly. "And no one thought to wake me? I love seeing you three get your derrieres handed to you." Virginia was too classy to talk about butts in English, clearly.

I rolled my eyes at her. Half the time our elderly ghost reminded me of a sassy teenager —and that was when she wasn't trying to kill us somehow, someway. I had to hand it to her. She didn't give up easily.

"Had I known a zombie was coming, I'd have done what I could to help," she added with a *humph.*

"Funny, I'm pretty sure you don't speak bird." Luna growled and crouched low as she faced Virginia.

"Nor do you, *dear*," the ghost said, mocking her former master's affectation.

"You've been spying on us," I countered. It wasn't a question.

Virginia shrugged. "Remember, you're the one who made it so that I can't leave this wretched place. Of course I'm spying. Problem is I've got nobody to tell."

I bit my lower lip and nodded. Virginia was right, of course. She couldn't talk to anyone who wasn't inside the four walls of this house. Meanwhile the cats and I knew better than to let unvetted strangers into our abode.

One thing was immediately clear: our zombie maker wasn't working with our ghost. On the one hand, that was good news. Nobody had unfettered access to us the way Virginia did.

But on the other hand?

I had no idea where to look next.

And something told me it would be much harder to defeat zombies if we didn't know when or where they'd be coming. Well, at least we'd had the last few weeks to rest up. A fight was definitely brewing, and judging from this morning's showdown, it wouldn't be one that we could easily win.

4

"Should we go do some research in Nocturna?" I asked the cats, refer-ring to the hidden fantasy city that was only accessible via an active witch's cauldron—or in our case, via the birdbath in the front yard where Merlin also brewed his potions as needed.

"We can't always run straight to Nocturna. There are other ways of solving things," my cat groused. One of his sharp teeth protruded over his bottom lip, giving him an irritated yet comical appearance.

"So says the guy who has a certain Tom cat looking to take him down," Luna teased. One thing I'd learned quickly while hanging around these two was that cats' love lives were even more complicated than humans'. First they'd broken up to pursue their magic, then they'd become sworn enemies, had a big showdown, got back together suddenly, and now kittens were on the way. Merlin had also upset a few of Luna's other suitors who believed she'd made the wrong choice. One had even challenged Merlin to a magical duel, which the Maine Coon had foolishly accepted.

Returning to Nocturna meant risking Merlin's magic, because if he fought and lost, he'd have to spend forever without it. Unfortunately, Luna and I couldn't enter Nocturna without Merlin since he was the only active witch. And if he lost his magic, not only would we be permanently locked out of the city, but we'd also be sitting ducks on this side of the cauldron. Whatever supernatural entity was after us now might not stop pursuing us if we lost our only source of magic, even though we'd be completely helpless without it.

And that's what made this whole thing so frustrating. Our zombie master was literally manipulating life and death. I preferred to remain among the living, thank you very much.

I wrung my hands as I glanced from one cat to the other. "If not Nocturna, then where do we start? Do we try to capture one of the zombies and ask it what it knows?"

Virginia drifted closer to me, and I flapped my hand as if she were a foul smell I could send floating in the other direction.

She simply laughed and moved in even closer. "You only bested me out of stupid luck. Don't expect to get so lucky again. There's no way someone as ill-equipped as you—all three of you—could possibly take out a master of the undead. Soon I won't be the only ghost around here, mark my words."

Luna raised her hackles and swiped at the air. "Go away, you nuisance! The only weak one here is you. You signed your own death warrant when you decided to betray me in your quest for power. And you have no one to blame but yourself, and possibly that awful illusion witch."

Merlin nodded thoughtfully, but I could tell something had distracted him. "We can capture a zombie, yes, but there's no point in keeping it alive—erm, animated. They aren't intelligent enough to do anything more than go after their mark. They're disposable. The perfect henchmen, because they won't get distracted and they won't betray their maker."

"You really think you stand a chance, don't you?" Virginia laughed even louder.

Merlin spun to face her, anger glowing in his green eyes. "Quiet, or I'll eat you, too!"

Virginia opened her mouth to say something, but Merlin continued to glare at her with all the hostility he could muster, which just so happened to be quite a lot.

She sighed and floated toward the edge of the room. She stayed near enough to keep spying, but at least she'd removed herself from the active conversation.

"Do we think this could be Dash?" I asked the two cats. "It seemed like a pretty sure thing she'd be coming back to challenge us again. Is that what's happening here?"

"It's as good a guess as any, dear," Luna agreed before licking her paw and rubbing it over her forehead.

"She could be anywhere, though," I pointed out. "She could look like anyone or anything.

How will we know when we've found her?" Dash's ability to manipulate others' perception is what had allowed her to get so close to us the first time around.

"We won't know," Merlin said stonily. "At least not at first. But I'm pretty sure she wants us alive. At least long enough for her to carry out whatever plans she has for us. I say we let her capture us, and then take it from there."

"Darling," Luna gasped, stomping her front paw down on the ground and drawing a startled expression from both of us. "That's incredibly dangerous! Think of the kittens!"

"I am thinking of the kittens, which is why I need you to stay here." Merlin licked Luna's forehead and then marched over to the door and waited, all the while wagging his tail impatiently.

"C'mon, Gracie," he called in a voice that brooked no argument. "The sooner we get this started, the sooner we can finish it, once and for all."

I didn't want to put myself into the middle of their argument, but we didn't have a better plan for sussing out our zombie wrangler and I couldn't bear to stand by and do nothing while we waited for him or her to strike again.

I sighed and offered Luna an apologetic glance as I slipped my feet into a pair of shoes, grabbed my keys, and followed Merlin outside.

"Let's go catch ourselves a bad guy," I said once I'd securely closed the door behind us.

"Actually," Merlin said with a smug grin. "We're going to let a bad guy catch us, instead."

I nodded and followed my cat down the street with no idea whether our slapdash plan would work at all.

5

I strolled down the street, trying to appear casual despite the giant housecat walking determinedly at my side.

"What should I be doing?" I mumbled to Merlin when I was sure nobody was looking our way.

"Act... natural," he said through a closed mouth.

We turned the corner and found old Mrs. Harkness watering her begonias with a pleasant smile on her face.

"Good morning, Grace!" she chimed. "And good morning to your furry little companion there, too."

I waggled my fingers in a wave and put on my best smile. "Yes, it's a great morning!" I called back.

"I said *act natural,*" Merlin hissed from below.

"What's that, sugar?" Mrs. Harkness responded with a furrowed brow as she shut off the hose and blinked into the sun.

"Oh, j-j-just admiring the natural beauty of the day!" I said, quickening my pace before she could figure out who'd really spoken.

I waited until we were an entire block away before speaking again. "That was too close." I kneeled down to stroke Merlin's head and kept my voice low. Hopefully any passers-by would just think I was cooing over my pet. "You shouldn't talk while we're outside. Anyone could be listening."

Merlin winked at me, and I straightened back to a standing position, ready to continue on our way.

But then Merlin let out a terrible yowl and kicked up his back feet in distress.

I reached down to pet him, but he swatted at my hand. "LU! NA!" he half shouted, half meowed.

I glanced down the block, and sure enough, I spotted a tiny white blur on the horizon. I don't think I'd ever seen Luna move so fast, but I also had no doubts it was her, especially given Merlin's unhappy reaction.

When she caught up with us, she plopped her butt on the ground right in front of Merlin.

"I told you to stay home!" he seethed.

"And I told you I'm not sitting this one out," she shot back in a raspy whisper.

"And I told you we need to avoid talking while we're outside where anyone could hear."

"You didn't tell me that, dear," Luna pouted. "See, I'm already missing things. I refuse to be written out of our adventures just because I'm about to become a mom. We work best as a team. You need me."

"Okay, but seriously, stop talking while we're in public!" I hissed as a beat-up minivan rolled past us. The driver gawked at me like I was some kind of crazy person, and he was absolutely right.

Once he passed, Luna let out a high-pitched meow and rubbed her face against my hand—to signal her agreement, I supposed. Well, at least one of them saw things my way.

And Luna was right, too. She'd been an integral part of our adventures so far, and we wouldn't have escaped either alive without her help.

Merlin stared at us both with wide green eyes, flicking his tail back and forth unhappily. He didn't speak again, though, so I guess that meant he agreed to keep mum for a bit.

"I have no idea where I'm going," I admitted in a whisper, crouching low again. "Can one of you take the lead?"

Luna meowed and trotted ahead, turning back only for a second to make sure we followed.

Merlin emitted a low rumble, but otherwise fell in line. He hated when he wasn't the one in charge, not that such a thing happened very often.

Luna set a pace much faster than my normal gait, and after a few more blocks I found myself breathing heavy as sweat beaded at my hairline.

"This isn't working," I complained. "Nobody is paying any attention to us."

Merlin opened his mouth, ready to come at

me with either an "I told you so," or "serves you right for trying to silence my voice."

"Oh, I wouldn't say nobody," a smooth voice responded from a nearby azalea shrub before Merlin could speak. All the words ran together with no breaths in between, creating a creepy, snake-like sound. Still, even though I couldn't immediately place it, I knew I'd heard this voice before. I mean, how could I forget something so eerily distinct?

Luna charged straight into the bush while Merlin hung back on the sidewalk with me. Soft feline voices whispered back and forth, and a few moments later Luna peeped her little white face out and motioned for Merlin and me to come closer.

Oh, I really hoped the owner of this azalea didn't make an appearance anytime soon, because I had no idea how I'd explain my way out of this one. Merlin entered the bush easily, but I had to drop to my hands and knees and bring my face close to the earth to see through the tangle of leaves and branches.

Three glowing pairs of eyes met mine— blue, green, and yellow. When it came to the new arrival, I couldn't see anything more than

those bright, sun-like eyes, but that was
enough for me to place him.

Mr. Fluffikins had arrived.

Which meant we definitely had trouble on
our hands.

6

"*I* was called to investigate a disturbance in the area," the black cat explained.

We first met Fluffikins after Merlin had summoned lightning in the house and blasted a hole straight through the roof. I didn't have the money to fix it, and Merlin didn't have the correct type of magic, so he and Luna phased in and out of various neighborhoods around Southern Georgia until they found Mr. Fluffikins.

His magic was different than what Merlin's was or what Luna's had been. Instead of being tied to a particular element in nature, Fluffikins wielded a special kind of magic generated from the earth's core, and with it, he could do almost anything.

He used his elite skills to manage a team of mixed paranormals in the nearby town of Beech Grove. While small, Beech Grove served as the magical hub for this region of the state, which made the little black cat crouched before us the single most powerful magical being for miles. If he'd been called in to investigate a disturbance himself, then that definitely meant it was something big.

I bit my lower lip, trying to keep all the questions I wanted to ask from tumbling out one after the other.

As I'd learned at Merlin and Luna's wedding, Fluffikins was all about ceremony and precedent. He wanted things done a certain way—nay, *demanded* they be done a certain way. And when it came to magical hierarchy, my cat outranked me mightily.

Sure enough, Merlin took the lead for our side of the conversation, holding his nose high to show that the other cat didn't intimidate him, even though that may not have been true. "Might that disturbance be related to zombies?"

Fluffikins tilted his head to the side; his eyes appeared to float in the darkness. "Zombies, no. Nothing so terrible as that."

"Well..." Merlin shifted his weight from paw to paw before continued. "I'll have you know that we got attacked by a zombie robin this morning and have reason to believe more will be on the way."

"More? Are you sure it wasn't just a one-off? A new magic user practicing the life-share spell that accidentally transferred it to the wrong entity?"

"We're sure," Luna answered with a grave expression.

"Well, since I'm already here, do you need my help?" Fluffikins offered. "It's the least I can do while I search for my mark."

"Who's your mark?" I asked, unable to hold back my curiosity.

Fluffikins let out a weary sigh. "It's an unfortunate thing. A young vampire is running rampant in your town. He risks exposing all of magical kind to the humans due to his recklessness."

"I haven't noticed anything unusual," I said

with a shrug. "Maybe it's not as bad as you think."

"We've been lucky so far, but if he isn't reined in soon, we'll have quite the situation on our hands." He paused and turned away from me, redirecting his attention on the highest-ranking individual here. "Merlin, do you need my help handling your zombies?"

My cat sniffed the air and shook his head. "Thanks, but no. We are fully capable of dealing with this on our—"

"*CHEE TEE TEEE YAAAAAH!*" A loud cry rent the air unlike anything I'd ever heard before. Shortly after, a small projectile shot through the bush and landed before us.

It rose on two legs, expertly shaking off the force of the impact, then turned toward Merlin with murder in its dark, glistening eyes.

"CHYAHHHHHH!" It belted out again, throwing itself at the Maine Coon's face.

Merlin staggered backward, but his tiny attacker grabbed onto his whiskers and clung tight, refusing to be shaken away.

Luna and Fluffikins both jumped into action. Luna hurled herself at the invader, slashing out with sharp claws in an urgent desire to defend her mate.

Mr. Fluffikins summoned a swirling pink tendril of magic and used it to lasso the creature and pry it away from Merlin. Once captured, he held it up for a closer inspection.

The little thing hissed and snarled, trying desperately to break free. When Fluffikins didn't let it go, the creature began to gnaw at his shoulder.

That's when I recognized the creature for what it was—a squirrel. No sooner had I figured that out than the attack squirrel broke his arm clear off and slipped from a surprised Fluffikins's magical grasp.

He bounded out of the bush and screamed again. *"TCHI-TCHI-TCHIIIIIYA!"*

Mr. Fluffikins spun in a circle, then sent a burst of magic straight into the air. It exploded around us, and I threw my hands over my head defensively.

"No one in a one-block radius will see or hear us, but we must dispose of this vile creature quickly!" he shouted. And just like that, all three cats bounded from the bush, ready for one heck of a fight.

*S*quirrels rained down from above, a veritable army descending from the sky—or at least from a nearby tree branch. Being that I was stuck on my hands and knees with my head pushed into a bush, I found myself completely at their mercy.

Tiny, clawed hands scraped at my back, and —oh—how it hurt! I backed out of that azalea as quickly as I could and scrabbled to my feet, but the tiny fiends hung on tight.

Merlin, Luna, and Mr. Fluffikins charged forth and fell upon the squirrels who'd attached themselves to me.

But more kept coming in a steady wave. Black, gray, brown, even red squirrels, all with crazed looks in their eyes, all determined to tear us to shreds.

And honestly I didn't know how to fight them. Nor did I want to. I'd always loved watching the playful squirrels who came to snack at the bird feeder in our backyard.

While just as agile, these squirrels were decidedly different. Unhinged. And given the spectacle the first one had treated us to, I was willing to bet they were also undead. It seemed our zombie master had found us, which meant the plan had worked. In hindsight, it was a horrible plan.

Another worry zoomed to mind. Could undead squirrels still spread rabies? I'd have to add visiting the hospital for a screening to my long list of things to do later that day, providing we even survived this heckin' crazy battle.

One of the little bucktoothed monsters sunk his teeth into my neck, and I roared in pain. Served me right for getting so lost in my thoughts when I should have been present in the moment.

I'd only just shook off the last squirrel when another assaulted me and a turbocharged acorn thwapped into the side of my head.

What the...? I turned sharply to the side as a half dozen more nuts and assorted other projectiles slammed into my face.

Oh, that did it!

Gone were my inhibitions about hurting the cute little animals. They were already dead-ish anyway, and if I didn't fight back, then one of the cats or I could follow in that unfortunate wake.

Ms. Gracie Springs was no pushover, no sirree!

I began to stomp around, trying to crush the little monsters beneath my feet. However, not even that could keep them down. The flattened beasts rose again, slithering on their bellies as they sought out their revenge.

"There's too many!" Merlin shouted. "I can't eat them all!"

Luna's gorgeous white fur was streaked with blood as she continued to bite and claw and pounce. Even Fluffikins looked worse for wear as he wielded his magic like a whip to keep the undead hoard at a distance.

A roaring engine sounded somewhere out

of sight. I jerked my head toward the sound, and one of the combatants used that opportunity to scamper up my side and plant itself on top of my head.

I screamed and threw my hands up, desperately trying to roust the thing before he could chomp down and possibly give me a permanent scar for all to see.

The noisy engine grew louder and louder as the vehicle approached. Whoever it was would see us embroiled in battle: woman and cats versus angry, deformed squirrels. How was I supposed to explain this one away?

Wait, no. Mr. Fluffikins had cast a shield. Our secret was safe, but were we? There were only four of us, and the zombie master seemed to have an endless army of squirrels at his command. Were we sure it was Dash? That whoever this was wanted us alive?

Vroom, vroom. The noisy engine drew closer and closer before turning a sharp corner and revealing a motorcycle and helmeted rider.

A second squirrel climbed onto my head and yanked at my ponytail. I glanced toward Merlin, but he was now pinned like Gulliver waking up on the island of the Lilliputians. It took two dozen of the smaller creatures to hold him down, but they'd managed to overpower him by working together.

The bike revved and picked up speed.

I whipped my head toward the sound, watching in horror as it lifted up onto the side-walk, coming straight for us with no signs of slowing down.

We may be protected from prying eyes and ears by Fluffikins's shield, but that wouldn't stop the motorcycle from crashing into us. The rider didn't even know he was in danger.

This was it. If the speeding bike didn't kill me, the zombie squirrels would.

Oh, of all the ways to die!

8

*T*he motorcycle jerked to the side, only narrowly missing me as it took out several of the squirrel fighters, its thick rubber tires driving their little bodies into the cement. Still, the furry zombies twitched and attempted to pry themselves from the ground.

The bike reversed, then came to a stop a few feet away from me. The rider lifted his visor to reveal the sharp features of my fellow barista and kind of friend, Drake.

"Grab the cats and hop on," he shouted before dropping the visor once more.

Well, he didn't have to tell me twice, and I didn't have to tell the cats at all. We piled on, even as the remaining squirrels jumped at us and pelted us with acorns.

I briefly wondered how he'd managed to spot us despite the protective barrier, but I was both too shocked and too grateful to question this lucky circumstance. Besides, magic was weird when it came to Drake. This wasn't the first time he'd been able to do what others couldn't.

"Hang on tight!" Drake revved the engine and the bike jolted to life.

The remaining squirrels cried and chirruped, moving impossibly fast in their pursuit.

We were definitely out of the warded bubble now, which meant magical and non-magical alike would be able to see our panicked departure and the angry animal mob giving chase.

Drake kicked things up, moving at least double the legal speed limit now—or at least that's what it felt like to my unpracticed mind.

Merlin and Luna both dug their nails into me as we took a sharp turn.

Mr. Fluffikins produced some kind of swirly pink magic that, while just hardly visible, firmly glued him to the bike. I wished he would have taken the time to also help my cats, but no.

My poor thighs!

We zoomed past my house, and I moved one of my hands from Drake's waist to squeeze at his shoulder. "Aren't we going to stop?"

"No way!" he yelled back, his voice just barely audible over the roaring engine and rushing wind. "Those little suckers looked like they meant business. I'm getting you as far away from here as possible." Or at least I think that's what he said.

We drove with only the sounds of the engine and speeding wind to keep us company. After about twenty minutes, we at last came to a stop outside of a stylish bungalow at the edge of town.

"Welcome to *mi casa,*" Drake announced, parking the bike in the driveway next to a Segway of all things.

"Thanks," I muttered breathlessly. The world felt like it was still rushing past me even though I stood on solid pavement once more.

Drake lifted his helmet to reveal a swash of hair styled to within an inch of its life with hard, spiky gel. "I'm glad I didn't miss that fight. Zombie squirrels? Who knew such a thing even existed? I mean, I'd hoped but..."

"Wait, how did you know they were zombies?" I asked, my mouth gaping open in shock.

He bent down to check his hair in one of the bike's mirrors and winked at himself. "Oh, you know. I like to know a little bit about a lot of bit. Zombies included. And that vacant expression in their eyes was a dead giveaway."

"Undead," I murmured, unable to help the small smile that played at my lips. Leave it to Drake to bring his signature levity to any situation.

"Why were they attacking you, anyway?" he asked with an inquisitive gaze, turning his full attention to me now that he knew his hair still looked the way he wanted.

"Um..." I started, then immediately stopped.

Because seriously, how could I even begin to explain? Earlier, he'd seen Virginia's ghost and found out that my cats were magical and could talk, but we'd given him a special potion to wipe his memory and cover our tracks.

Despite our best efforts, though, he refused to attribute all the strange things that had happened that night to a wild dream as we had planned. He knew something was up, which meant I had to tread lightly here.

But how could I possibly explain away a homicidal squirrel hoard?

Mr. Fluffikins saved me from having to explain myself when he hopped away from the bike and rounded on Drake. "Why, if it isn't just the man I was looking for," he said with an unhappy smile splashed across his face.

"What's up, little cat dude?" Drake asked with a laugh, leading us all through his garage and into his home.

Fluffikins kept his tail low and curled at the end. "I'm here to get you registered with your local supernatural board. It seems you've been creating quite a few issues during your nocturnal wanderings."

Drake stopped inside the doorway and starcd at the bossy black cat through squinted eyes. "Come again now?"

Fluffikins entered behind him and then hopped up onto the counter, refusing to break eye contact with Drake. "Have you registered? If not, I'm taking you in right now."

Luna, Merlin, and I stood just outside the door, watching the scene unfold with wide eyes. I think we realized what was happening before Drake did.

"Why would I need to register?" he asked with a nervous chuckle. "You said this was for a supernatural board? That's great and everything, like, fine I'll register, but I'm not supernatural."

Mr. Fluffikins sighed. "Please don't tell me you don't even know what you are."

Drake dipped his hands into his pockets and rocked on his heels. "I'm just an average-ish guy living off his trust fund and keeping busy."

The boss cat let out a dry laugh. "Average guy? Not even close."

All eyes were on Mr. Fluffikins. Nobody spoke. We were all waiting to see whether Drake would figure this out on his own.

What a revelation. I'd always known something was off about Drake, but this?

My friend shook his head and crossed his arms over his chest. "Sorry, I don't follow."

Fluffikins shook his head and sighed. When he looked up again, he spoke slowly, as if to an imbecile.

If Drake was offended, he didn't show it.

"You are a supernatural creature and need to register with the board."

"Oh yeah?"

We all nodded.

"And what kind of supernatural creature am I, Mr. Pussy Cat?"

"A vampire," Fluffikins said around a growl. "And don't you dare ever call me Mr. Pussy Cat again."

9

*D*rake took a step back and leaned into the wall. "No," he said, shaking his head. "That's not possible. I mean, I think I would know if I were a vampire."

I glanced toward Merlin who was rolling his eyes.

Luna at least showed some compassion but didn't speak a word.

"It's okay, Drake. Really. You're still you," I offered with a small smile.

Drake groaned and shook his head. "No. I'm not. I can't be."

Mr. Fluffikins lifted a paw and extended one claw. "Looks like I need to convince you, so here we go. Let's start with the easy stuff. Do you ever just know something that you shouldn't? Like memories of things that haven't actually happened?"

Drake nodded mutely, and Fluffikins extended a second claw.

"And do you ever wake up somewhere with no recollection of how you got there?" he pushed further.

Drake nodded again.

Fluffikins added a third claw to his furry fist. "Do you have an insatiable craving for wealth and knowledge?"

Drake said nothing.

"You know a little bit about a lot of bit," I said, quoting him back to himself. "And you do live off a trust fund."

Drake's entire face had drained of color by now, giving him a much more vampirish appearance than before. Honestly, I'd never seen him look so unsettled, not even when Virginia's ghost was actively trying to murder us. I watched now as his hands groped at the wall, unable to gain purchase.

When he spoke again, his voice came out broken and pitchy. "B-b-but I don't drink blood. I would never ever do such a thing!"

Fluffikins's claws retreated back into his paw, and he set his foot on the tile floor. "Did I say anything about drinking blood?" he asked with a low growl. He then turned to me with a peeved-off look. "You humans and your stupid lore. You've set vampires back hundreds of years, thanks to your so-called entertainment. Hundreds of years, that's when they actually did drink blood. It's been ages!"

"I'm s-s-sorry," I muttered, more a question than a declaration. Why was he blaming me for this when I was the only one here who was actually trying to help him!

"Normally new vampires aren't left on their own. Something must have gone wrong with your turning." The black cat blinked slowly while watching the newly revealed vampire for his reaction.

"So I wasn't born a vampire?" Drake's voice still squeaked like a preteen as he pushed out words in a hurry. "My mom and dad aren't—"

"Heavens no, nobody is born a vampire. How ridiculous!" Now it was Mr. Fluffikins who was rolling his eyes. Cats were not the most patient creatures, something I'd learned early on in my employ as a familiar.

But Drake didn't know any better. Even if he'd been okay with my magical stuff, this was different. He'd just found out that he was a monster, and one who had been unintentionally causing havoc at that.

He sank to the floor, cradling his head in his hands. "I'm dead," he murmured. "I'm legit dead."

"Well, technically you're undead," Fluffikins clarified with a sniff.

"Just like those squirrels," Merlin added with a laugh.

Luna shot him an irritated glance. "Go gentle on him, dear. Can't you see how upset he is already?"

Fluffikins had started laughing, too, but managed to pull himself together quickly. "If you're friends with this guy, how did you not figure out what he was?" he asked me.

"That's a good question," I said, turning my eyes back to Merlin.

He puffed up defensively. "What? I can't know everything about everything, okay? I knew something was up with the guy, but most vampires are loud and proud. How was I supposed to know what he was when even he didn't?"

Well, he had a point there.

"Settle down, you." Luna brushed up against Merlin's side and purred, nuzzling him until he at last deflated.

"You three will be able to see yourselves home from here, right?" the boss cat asked Merlin, then walked up to a gently sobbing Drake. "You need to come with me."

He continued to cry, not acknowledging Fluffikins or any of the rest of us. As for me, I didn't know exactly what Mr. Fluffikins did on a day to day, but I knew he wasn't used to taking no for an answer. And I also knew he would be unlikely to back down now.

Sure enough, the black cat extended his claws and tapped at Drake's arm. "Did you hear me, vampire? I need you to—"

"Perhaps we could be a little more delicate with him?" I suggested. "And maybe since you're here, you can help us with our zombie problem? I mean you did offer earlier. Let's take a break from vampires and talk zombies. Sound good?"

He shook his head from side to side. "That

was before I'd found my charge. As you can see, I got what I came for and now I need to get back to Beech Grove. Many pressing matters await the vampire and me there."

"Are you kidding me right now?" Luna piped up. It wasn't like her to go on the offensive like this, but apparently she'd been pushed too far. "You're the diplomat for this entire region, and you're not at all worried about a zombie invasion?"

"It was very clear they were coming for you and you alone, so it's not an issue that takes precedence. This guy on the other hand..." He jerked his head toward Drake. "He's been causing trouble all across Peach Plains. We need to rein him in, and ASAP, or risk the exposure of our kind."

"So what? You're just going to let us die at the hands of this rogue zombie master?" I exploded, glaring at the cat with all the hostility I could muster.

"Tell you what," Fluffikins said with a sigh. "Submit your request in writing, and the board will get back to you in 5-10 business days."

I nodded dumbly. It was the only way to keep from screaming at the helpless jerk.

Fluffikins tapped Drake with his claws again and cleared his throat. "Now are you coming with me or what?"

Drake sobbed and moaned but didn't offer any words in response.

"Fine, then. We'll do it the hard way," Mr. Fluffikins bit out, and then both he and Drake disappeared in a swirl of sparkling pink magic.

10

The three of us that weren't swept up by Mr. Fluffikins's flash magic marched out of the house and into Drake's backyard. Once there, Merlin blinked twice to take us home. It was always easier for him to navigate outdoors rather than from inside an unfamiliar place.

"Well, a fat load of good that did us," the Maine Coon grumbled before padding over to his water dish for a quick drink.

"It was a good plan, dear. Really," Luna coaxed. "But Drake rescued us before our zombie master could capture us."

"I'm very angry with you," Merlin said to

his wife after licking a few errant drops of water from his lips.

Her tail shot straight up, then arched forward at a sharp angle. "Don't be. I'm fine."

Merlin's tail immediately rearranged itself into the same position. "I said it would be dangerous and that you should stay back, but you refused to listen. Look what happened! You could have been hurt. One of the kittens could have been hurt!"

"I'm not a delicate flower, and I'm not a child," Luna hissed as she stood ramrod straight, refusing to budge.

"Oh, you think—"

"Enough!" I cut in. "We're all on the same side here. If we fight among ourselves, we don't stand a chance. As it is, we have no idea what we're doing. Let's not make this even harder than it already is."

Luna relaxed her stance and dipped her head apologetically. "You're right, dear. Of course, you're right."

Even though Merlin was technically my boss, I decided to take charge of the situation. It was the only way we'd make any progress at all. "Merlin, I know you just want to keep your family safe, but you have to let Luna decide for herself what that entails. You know she wouldn't knowingly put herself or the kittens in danger. She's smart and strong, and we need her help if she's willing to give it."

Neither cat said anything, but at least they didn't argue with my hasty decree.

After a few moments of tense silence, I went on. "Okay, our first plan wasn't exactly a success, so I think it's time to make a new one. I know you're *catsona non grata* in Nocturna, Merlin, but I really think that's where we ought to go next. I mean, we think our zombie master may be Dash, and we know Dash is interested in our bloodlines."

"We already met with the blood witch. We know exactly what we are and how we're connected." Merlin still stood in an awkward stance, though he had lowered his tail to a less hostile position.

When I shook my head to disagree, his tail shot back up into that mean forward hook.

I sighed. Why did everything have to be a battle for dominance? I just wanted to figure out this zombie thing before we were attacked again. If we could avoid that, I'd be one happy lady.

Still, I proceeded carefully. "Clearly there's something more that we're missing. I think we should go back and see if we can find out what that is."

Luna stretched out her back legs as she moved toward me. "And before you say anything, I'm coming, too."

"Neither of you can go if I refuse to take you there," Merlin pointed out with a half-hearted snarl. He'd already begun to deflate again.

"Then it's a good thing you're not refusing," I said with a cheeky grin.

"What about Tom and his cronies?" Merlin asked. "They're probably still looking for me so we can finish our duel."

More than a month had passed since that run-in, but I knew very well that cats could hold grudges for longer that. "Can't you use magic to change your appearance?" I suggested with a shrug.

"I'm a sky witch, and you know that. Illusions are out of my wheelhouse." He yawned and fell over onto his side dramatically.

"I can give you a makeover if you want?"

"Hard pass." Merlin jumped up and stalked down the hall.

"Where are you going?" I called after him.

"The portal to Nocturna doesn't open until sundown. I'm taking a nap," came his mumbled reply.

Luna yawned. "That sounds like a good idea," she said before heading through the cat flap and to her favorite spot in the rear garden.

That just left me, alone in the kitchen.

Maybe I could pound out some work on my master's thesis, make something of this day yet.

"I see you're still alive and well. How awful for me," a ghostly Virginia droned as she phased through the wall and came to hover before me.

Yeah, no. I was not dealing with her if I could avoid it.

I grabbed my keys and left the house in a hurry.

I had no idea where I was going, but hopefully I could at least get a few hours of peace and quiet before diving even deeper into this zombie adventure of ours.

11

*M*y life was in a sad state, considering the only place I could think to go was my place of work, Harold's House of Coffee. No, I was not scheduled that day. Yes, my social life had probably hit rock bottom.

In truth, I hadn't taken the time to get to know many people since relocating to Elderberry Heights. All my family was back home in Michigan, other than Grandma Grace who'd moved to the Florida Keys. I'd left my friends back in my old college town, and all my new neighbors had a good forty years on me.

My boss Kelley had become a good friend over the last couple months, though. I'd supported her through her father's death and the resulting murder investigation and stayed by her side as she rebranded Harold's House of Coffee to serve all pumpkin spice lattes all the time.

She was also dating Drake, which made her the perfect person to mine for some info about him and the nighttime troubles Mr. Fluffikins had spoken of.

As far as I knew, Kelley was one-hundred percent certified human. But I'd assumed that Drake had been, too.

Who even knew anymore?

"Hey, girl. What can I get you?" Kelley sang out the moment I walked into the cafe.

"Just a hot tea. Thanks." I'd never been much of a tea drinker, but I'd recently become very anti-PSL. Too much of a good thing and all that. It was easier to pretend I didn't want coffee than to hurt Kelley's feelings. Because if I refused to accept her offer of a free drink, she'd just go ahead and serve me up whatever new concoction she was testing for the masses. Ergo, my request for hot tea despite the hot weather.

"How's today been?" I asked when she slid

a mug of nearly boiling water to me over the counter. I casually plucked a bag of hibiscus tea from the display and dunked it into my cup.

"Busy as usual," she answered with a bright smile.

"Hey, have you heard anything from Drake?" *Real smooth, Gracie!* It was no small wonder I'd managed to survive all my recent scrapes, given how poor my people skills could be at times. Then again, I was mostly dealing with cats and other supernatural types lately.

Kelley shook her head. "Not since this morning when we texted hello. Why? Is something up?"

"Oh, yeah. I mean, no. Everything's fine!" I hurried to reassure her as I poured a couple packets of sugar into my mug and grabbed a stir stick. I kept my mouth pressed in a firm line as I finished preparing my drink. Why hadn't I at least attempted to come up with a plan on my way over here?

After mentally scolding myself once more for good measure, I raised my eyes to meet Kelley's and asked, "He's just been acting a little weird lately. Don't you think?"

"Weird how?" she said distractedly as she

got to work making an iced drink for a customer.

"It's hard to describe," I ventured, not wanting to give away any of Drake's or my secrets. "Just, you know, weird."

Kelley tilted her head to the side as she thought, all while effortlessly engaging the blender. "Well, Drake's always been different. That's why I like him so much."

"You're right," I said, disparaged at how quickly I'd reached a dead end. "We shouldn't be surprised by anything he does."

"Yeah, like how he bought that Segway for no rhyme or reason," she said with a giggle.

"And the motorcycle," I added with a laugh.

Kelley shot me a silly look. "Yeah, guess which one of those two I like better." She shuddered, then poured the blended drink into a tall glass. "Segways really aren't meant for two people, but that didn't stop him from picking me up for our date using that thing last week."

I joined her in laughter, and it felt great to occupy my mind with something so frivolous for a change. We chatted about other things for a few minutes, but I knew I shouldn't stay too long and disrupt her work, especially given the fact that Harold's was always busy and needed all hands on deck.

"Well, I should probably--"

"Hold that thought!" Kelley interrupted, fishing her phone out of her apron. I hadn't heard it chime, but that wasn't exactly surprising since she tended to keep it on silent mode.

"Oh, hey, it's Drake!" she announced with a giddy grin, but as she read on her face rearranged itself into a frown. "He says he's going to be out of town for a few days and wanted to know if I could find someone to cover his shifts."

Kelley lowered the phone but continued to stare blankly where it had been. "We're supposed to go on a date tonight, but apparently he's already left. He didn't even say why."

"Maybe he's planning a surprise for you," I said, forcing a fresh wave of enthusiasm. Of course, I knew the truth about Drake's sudden disappearance. If I saw him before she did, I'd have to tell him to do something special for Kelley or to risk losing her as his girlfriend. Then again, if he was truly a vampire, maybe she was better off without him.

"Or he's cheating," Kelley said with a groan.

"No! He would never!" I reached over the counter and squeezed my friend's arm reassuringly.

"You did say he was acting weird lately. Do you know something I don't?" She raised an eyebrow my way.

"No, no, no. No way! I didn't mean that at all. Drake is crazy about you. Don't doubt that for a second. Anyway, I got to go."

And I rushed out of there as fast as I could without actually breaking into a run. Definitely not my finest moment.

12

*A*fter leaving the coffee shop, I drove around town for about an hour trying to gather my thoughts. During the relatively peaceful past few weeks, I'd begun to fantasize about getting back to a normal life. I'd actually thought that danger *wouldn't* be waiting around every corner, that I *wouldn't* have to strain so hard to keep my cat's magical world a secret.

Oh, how very wrong I'd been.

The more I thought, the more I despaired the current state of my life. I mean, what was the point in even finishing my master's degree at this point? It's not like I'd ever be able to get a normal job, not so long as I had my responsibilities as a familiar.

I'd once flirted with the idea of going even deeper into my education to land a doctorate. I loved school and would have enjoyed being a professor. But how could I ever truly make myself available to my students and colleagues if the enormity of my cat's secret always came first?

At least now I had an understanding boss at the coffee shop. I still couldn't summon the time or the passion needed to finish off my half-done thesis. What made me think I could take things to the next level with a doctoral dissertation? Or add classes on top of my current off-balance load?

Then there was the glaringly painful fact that I'd obviously never be able to fall in love, get married, have kids—all the things I didn't want now but knew I'd desire one day.

My cat and his magical needs always had to come first. Which meant I always had to come last.

I loved Merlin and Luna and knew I'd be crazy for their kittens, but what would happen if I ever wanted more?

Yeah, I probably shouldn't have been so fixated on the future, seeing as I didn't know whether we'd survive our current predicament —or the next one, or the one after that.

I was definitely getting ahead of myself, but I also couldn't help it.

It wasn't just me, though. I worried about Drake, too. A part of me had broken seeing him crumble to the floor like that.

I'd always viewed him as the ultimate chill guy, but even he had his limits. What would life be like for him now that he knew what he was?

I guess I should have been grateful that my problem was so small compared to his. Not only had Drake become a creature of the night, but he was all on his own. My magical servitude came with a whole family who loved me dearly, who had my back, no matter what.

It was with this one final thought in my head that I returned home, only to find one very angry kitty waiting at the kitchen table. "Oh, look who finally decided to show herself!" Merlin yowled. "Our water bowl has been empty for hours!"

"I was only gone an hour and a half," I said,

shaking my head and forcing myself to take slow, deep breaths so I wouldn't lose my cool.

"Likely story!" Merlin shouted back at me.

I bit my lip as I reached down to grab the cat's stainless steel water dish. I also reminded myself of the resolve I'd had in the car—this was my life, and these cats were my family. I loved them, even when they were working my last nerve. Still, I'd given up the chance to become a respected academic to work as the servant to one very spoiled kitty, regardless of the fact that he was also magical.

I finished filling the dish and set it on the table beside Merlin.

He took one hesitant drink, then sneezed and whispered, "It's not the right temperature. What are you doing to me here, Gracie?" proving that no matter how magical our world became, at the end of the day, Merlin was still an average, everyday cat, too.

"My apologies, your highness," I said with a mocking curtsy.

Merlin flicked his tail and narrowed his eyes at me for a moment before finally relenting with a sigh. "Fine, I'm sorry I'm being so rough on you. I'm having a hard time today, but I shouldn't be taking it out on you."

Wow, an actual apology. This would go down in history as one of my favorite days ever, despite the multiple attempts on my life via various undead creatures.

"Because of the zombies, you mean?" I asked tenderly as I picked up his bowl and carried it over to the sink. If he could apologize, then I could try a little harder to meet his needs, too.

"What?" Merlin stared across the room at a sunbeam he probably wished he was lying in rather than sitting here talking to me. "The zombies? Oh, no. I mean, sure they're a problem, but what really worries me is my Luna."

I set the bowl back down, and he came over to investigate. When Merlin decided the water was at the right temperature for consumption, he leaned forward and lapped it up heartily.

"I know you're only looking out for Luna," I said gently. Yes, I'd already made my opinion known on this matter, but it still weighed heavily on my cat's mind. I also felt like I needed to stick up for Luna here. Girl power and all that.

"Please don't tell me I need to apologize," Merlin mumbled, lifting his head momentarily.

"Well, that wouldn't be the worst idea."

"I already tried, but she wouldn't accept it."

Well, that was a shocker. "Are you sure?"

"Of course, I'm sure," Merlin snapped, then had the good sense to look ashamed for losing his temper. "Sorry, sorry. I know it's not your fault, but I'm not making any of this up. When I tried to apologize, Luna said she was too tired to argue anymore and asked if we could discuss it later."

"Oh," I said, not knowing what else I could offer. "Well, I'm sure everything will be fine. She probably just wants to deal with one thing at a time, and the zombies should definitely take precedence."

"Mmm-hmm," Merlin said, turning back to his water.

Yikes. I really hoped these two made up before the kittens arrived.

13

*W*hen at last night fell, the two cats and I marched out to the yard and straight over to Merlin's cauldron, aka the unassuming stone bird bath that served as his tie to all things magical, including the city of Nocturna.

We had to wait for a couple odd cars to drive past, but as soon as the coast was clear, we hightailed it to the cauldron. Merlin jumped up and splashed at the water, then motioned for me to jump on through.

This was only the second time I'd traveled via cauldron. My heart beat wildly as I plunged into the tiny opening to the next realm, but at least I managed to land on my feet. The cats joined me a few seconds later, and together we surveyed the bustling cobblestone streets of the old city. The buildings mimicked the Bavarian style and were made to accommodate cats rather than people. This gave everything an adorable fairy-tale quality, and I found it quite enchanting.

"Well, this is your plan, so what next?" Merlin asked, beaming up at me. It seemed our little talk in the kitchen had softened his demeanor some, thank goodness.

"We should see the blood witch," Luna said. It wasn't like her to interrupt, but I understood that tensions were high between her and Merlin. She probably just wanted to get this little trip finished as quickly as possible.

I nodded. "Yes, that's what I was going to say, too."

"Then let's go." Luna trotted down the cobblestone walkway, leaving us to follow.

Merlin and I exchanged curious glances before following after her. The sooner we got this over with, the sooner we could find a way to exterminate our zombie problem once and for all.

As we strolled through the darkened streets

of Nocturna, a few friendly cats called out to us. But nothing could stop Luna on her quest to reach our destination without delay.

As we rounded a corner, my toe caught a crack in the stone path, causing me to stumble and fall to my hands and knees.

"Are you all right?" Merlin asked, racing over to examine my skinned palms.

I let out a slow, shaky breath. It stung, but not bad enough for me to request magical aid. "I'm fine. It's just a bit hard to see without any lights," I offered as I slowly rose back to my feet.

"We have the moon to guide us," Luna said, tilting her head to the sky.

"Yes, but I don't have night vision like the two of you," I reminded her. The feline residents of Nocturna didn't need artificial light to see, which resulted in some paths being better lit than others. The one we had just turned onto had nary a lantern or lamppost to be seen.

"Right." Luna sat and waited for me to get my bearings before continuing on.

Our little party had almost made it to the old covered wagon where the flame-point

Siamese had his blood witch consultancy when a shadowy figure exploded from the alleyway and pounced on Merlin.

"Ah-ha! I knew you couldn't hide forever," a fat orange tabby snarled.

As a young Maine Coon, Merlin hadn't quite reached his full size. However, it was rare to find any other cats who were larger than him. Somehow, though, this chunky assailant seemed to outweigh him two to one.

"Get off him," I shouted and stomped my foot while Luna watched the scene unfold from several paces away.

"This scaredy cat owes me a duel," the orange chonker decreed, clueing me in to his exact identity.

"You're Tom," I said, pointing at him with an angry, shaking finger.

He flashed us a wide smile, showing off his pointed fangs. "Gee, what gave me away?"

"We have nothing to fight about," Merlin ground out, still trapped beneath the larger cat's bulk. "Luna made her choice, and it wasn't you."

"That's right! You tell him!" Luna called out

but kept her distance. "Now, please leave us. We have somewhere we need to be."

Tom scoffed at her request. "More important than this? I think not. I've been waiting weeks to put this guy in his place. Where you been, Merlin?"

"I have a life outside of Nocturna. And if memory serves, that's the whole problem in the first place." Merlin growled, then jerked his head to the side in a fast fake-out maneuver.

Tom toppled off him, giving Merlin the chance to escape his hold. Now both cats stood with their hackles raised, facing each other as they hissed wildly.

"You're jealous," Merlin bit out.

"Nah, I just don't like to see good things happen to bad cats," Tom countered. "Now, are we going to do this right here in the middle of the street, or what?"

"No, no." Merlin glanced toward Luna, and she nodded reassuringly. "I don't want anyone to get hurt. Let's take this to the fields."

Tom took a step back, then lowered himself to a sitting position. "I'm counting on you to be there," he said without taking his eyes from Merlin. "Five minutes, or you forfeit."

"You have my word," Merlin replied with a slight bow of his head.

And with that, Tom flashed a sinister smile, blinked twice, and disappeared into the night.

14

*L*una tiptoed over to Merlin and me. "Come. We have to be quick. There's still time to visit the blood witch before that thug returns."

Merlin mewed morosely and hung his head in shame. "I know you want to keep me from fighting, darling, but you know what happens if I forfeit."

"What happens?" I asked, feeling so out of the loop when it came to Nocturna's unique methods of conflict resolution.

"An All Paws Bulletin will go out to every single witch in the area. By refusing to fight, I'll have effectively surrendered my magic, and it is their right to take it from me." Merlin spoke passionlessly, as if he'd already accepted the worst possible outcome. It wasn't like him at all.

I shook my head emphatically. I'd believe in my cat enough for both of us, if that's what was needed. "We can't take a risk like that. Jeez. I'm so sorry, Merlin. I shouldn't have forced you to come back here. You tried to warn me."

The Maine Coon lifted a paw to silence me. "No. This is my fault entirely. I shouldn't have egged Tom on. I knew he was jealous, and still I took great pleasure rubbing my happiness in his face."

"But the blood witch..." Luna mewled pathetically.

"We can visit him once this is finished," I told her. I got that she didn't want Merlin to fight, but she could at least admit the hypocrisy rather than trying to act like she had other reasons for wanting to hold him back.

"What if you lose?" I asked Merlin somberly. As much as I didn't like it, we had to consider all possible outcomes. If Merlin lost the magical duel, he wouldn't die, but he would be left forever without his magic... And where would that leave me?

Merlin sighed. "Then I'm willing to bet the zombie master will be far less interested in what I do going forward."

"Well, that's one way to solve the problem, I guess." I forced a smile because I knew Merlin needed someone in his corner and Luna was oddly detached at the moment.

"In truth, I'm lucky that Tom didn't put out the APB the first time I disappeared. My guess is he'd find it far more satisfying to land a few good strikes of his own than to simply rob me of my magic due to a technicality."

I nodded slowly and glanced to Luna. Her blue eyes were wide as she took everything in, but still she remained silent—letting Merlin decide this one for himself, no doubt. Luna wanted Merlin to let her make her own decisions about what was safe versus what held more risk than acceptable, and now she was returning the favor.

"Is there anything we can do to help you get ready?" I asked after a brief moment of silence passed.

"Yes." He rose to all four feet and stretched. "I need you to remain as close to me as possible once I'm on the field while also keeping a safe distance from harm."

"How will I know what that is?" Too close and I'd put myself at risk. Too far away and I'd put Merlin at risk. This was not going to be easy, but it was the least I could do.

Merlin rubbed his head against my shin. "I don't know, but I'm trusting you to figure it out. Your presence will give me an advantage over Tom. He doesn't have a familiar, which means only I will have access to extra reserves if needed."

Oh, that was right!

Maybe we could win this thing after all. It could all come down to me. I could save Merlin's magic, and then once he defeated Tom fair and square, we wouldn't have to be afraid to return to Nocturna.

Finally my status as his familiar meant something; it gave me a bit of power—power which I fully intended to use for the greater good.

With any luck, Merlin would clinch a quick and painless victory, and we would still have the time we needed to visit the blood witch before the morning sun came out and put the city into a slumber.

If not, I'd need to be ready to bunk down in a town that wasn't made with humans in mind. And if Merlin lost his magic...

"I have a question," I blurted out. I didn't want to add to his anxiety over the pending duel, but I also needed to know.

Merlin plopped onto his rear and stared straight up at me. "Yes?"

"If you lose your magic, what happens to me?" I whispered meekly.

"Well, you remember what happened to Virginia when Luna cut hers off. It severed the tie. Just don't go chasing after the fleeing magic and try to avoid any wells, and you should be fine." He smiled half-heartedly, and I reached down to stroke his head.

"Oh, and there's one more thing you should probably know," he added sheepishly. "If I lose, then Luna and I will be able to leave with another cat's aid, but Gracie... You'll be stuck in Nocturna forever."

15

*S*tuck in Nocturna? But what would I do here? How could I make a life in a world to which I simply didn't belong?

"Can't another cat help me out, too?" I squeaked.

Merlin met my eye briefly, then looked away. "It's my blood to which you're tied. Our connection is what enables you to transport here. Without my magic, that connection is severed."

I gulped down the tangled knot of emotion that had formed in my throat. Merlin needed a strong second right now, not a liability. I had to push past my fears of what could be and do what he'd asked of me without any added doubts or hesitations on my part.

Merlin was a powerful witch. He'd proven that many times over.

He could win this.

In fact, he would.

Yeah, I just had to keep believing.

After all, he'd given me no reason to doubt his abilities before.

I clapped my hands together with more pep than I felt. "Then we'll just have to make sure you win this thing. Let's go!"

Merlin nodded slowly, then blinked twice, transporting the three of us to an open clearing far past town. An outcropping of buildings was just barely visible on the horizon, thanks to a ceiling of roaring fire that hung above us, illuminating the sky in all directions.

"Um, Merlin, what kind of witch is Tom?" I whispered, unable to tear my eyes away from the flames that threatened to come crashing down on us at any second.

"Volcano," he said with a tightly clenched jaw as he scanned the field for his rival.

I followed his line of sight but saw no one. Least of all Tom.

"Huh. Maybe he realized he bit off more than he could chew and decided to forfeit?" I suggested hopefully, but Merlin appeared unconvinced.

Above us, the sheet of fire undulated like a gentle wave, and I jerked my face up to watch the spectacle. As I watched, the waves began to crash angrily against an invisible barrier, then sloshed over its edges in massive plumes of lava.

Cracks appeared in the ground beneath my feet, and I jumped to the side to avoid being swallowed up by the sudden quake.

That tiny crack grew into a chasm as it raced off in the distance and exploded upward, creating a throne of dirt and rock.

The flames above reformed into a solid sheet and chased after the snaking fissure in a deadly dance. Both elements converged in a cyclone of grandeur born of destruction, and Tom leapt down from the throne, passing straight through the wall of fire.

"It's about time you showed up," the orange tabby said with a sinister smile. "And isn't it just like you to show up at the last possible minute?"

"Isn't it just like you to show up in a literal blaze of glory?" Merlin bit back with open contempt. "It'll take more than a few silly party tricks to impress me, though."

"Enough with the chit-chat. Your tail is mine, cat!" Tom chuckled cruelly as he raced toward Merlin on fast and steady paws.

I also moved swiftly toward the Maine Coon, knowing that the closer I clung to him, the easier it would be for him to put this guy in his place.

As Tom ran toward us, flames shot up behind him, propelling his thick mass even faster.

Merlin stood rooted to the spot as if entranced by the spectacle before him. And just when I was certain Tom would crash into him headfirst, Merlin spun around in a tight circle, kicking up a storm of his own.

A howling cyclone formed above him and launched toward Tom. By now the tabby had built up so much momentum that he couldn't stop himself in time. He crashed right into the maelstrom and was sucked inside, flames and all.

Merlin shouted something into the wind, but I couldn't hear it over the roaring gusts.

The twister spun faster and faster, lifted Merlin's opponent higher and higher. But Merlin wasn't done yet. He kicked his feet back behind him in a familiar maneuver. This was the power of his I most dreaded—after all, it had shot a hole straight through my roof.

He kicked faster and harder, again and again. His feet were a blur, and dust flew up, obscuring my view of the field.

And then from the sky...

CRACK!

A mighty bolt of lightning struck the cyclone, and I swear I saw Tom's skeleton flash before me, just like in the old-timey cartoons I'd watched on Saturday mornings as a child.

Merlin stumbled and fell forward. He'd just used his two most powerful spells back to back, and it had clearly taken a toll.

The tornado dissipated, and Tom thumped down onto the ground.

Neither cat moved, other than to take in giant racking breaths. Tom's magic sparked and flickered around his body.

Merlin did nothing.

"Merlin!" I called out to him. "You have to summon the rain. That's an easy one. You can do it!"

My witchy cat raised one paw to the sky but couldn't hold it up long enough to cast his magic.

I ran toward him. Maybe my touch could give him the strength he needed to finish this battle. I'd almost reached his side when a column of tightly packed mud shot straight from the earth, blocking me from moving any farther.

I darted to the side, but another pillar rose up to obscure that path, too.

"Merlin!" I screamed and pounded my fists against the earthen cage that had now ensnared me on all sides.

No, no, no!

If I didn't get to him—and fast—this could be the end for both of us...

16

I couldn't see anything except for occasional flashes of fire lighting the sky overhead. I screamed and pounded on the walls of mud that stretched high above me but couldn't break free.

"Surrender," Tom roared above it all.

I stopped screaming and fell quiet, waiting for Merlin's response.

"Ne... ver," he managed between pants.

"Your magic is mine," Tom rasped, proving that he, too, had taken quite the beating. "All I have to do is reach out and take it."

A terrifying silence stretched for what felt like ages.

What was happening? Was Merlin getting

back up to fight? Had Tom already relieved him of his magic? And what would happen to the magic once it was gone? Would it spill back into nature as Luna's had done, or could Tom truly wield both his and Merlin's at the same time?

"This is your last chance," Tom said with heated passion. "Get up and fight me like a cat, or give up now."

Something fell on my cheek, startling me. I jerked back just as another something hit my shoulder.

Rain!

Merlin had done it. He'd managed to bring the rain. It came hard and thick, beating down on me with increasing strength.

He was still in this!

The cats growled and hissed, continuing to fling magic at one another. Meanwhile, the rain began to pool at my feet, rising quickly from my knees to my shoulders, higher, higher.

I treaded water, waiting for the chance to pull myself out of my temporary prison and do whatever I could to help Merlin seize victory.

When at last I was able to peek above the enormous earthen wall, I caught a quick glimpse of Merlin with his claws poised at Tom's throat, ready to strike. I couldn't hold myself for long and fell back into the pool beneath me.

I pulled myself up a second time and clambered onto the narrow strip of land with shaky feet. I stood at least fifteen feet off the ground with no idea how to get safely down.

Both cats whipped their heads up and turned toward me.

A wicked smile flashed across Tom's striped face as he dodged to the right in a similar fakeout to the one Merlin had pulled on him in the alleyway. He wriggled free and summoned a massive ball of fire. A second later, he catapulted the thing straight toward me. I jumped to the ground, no longer concerned with how I would take the fall.

The important thing was to not die.

Just before I smacked into the earth, a gentle stream of wind caught me and lowered me gently. Merlin had saved my behind, literally.

Unfortunately, Tom had counted on Merlin shifting his attention to rescue me, and now their positions had reversed.

The enormous orange tabby straddled my Maine Coon, swinging his paws wildly as he batted at Merlin's face, chest, anywhere he could reach—attacking the very source of his magic.

"Oh, Merlin, did you think you could win?" he jeered as he struck out at Merlin and sent him flying.

This was all my fault. If I'd just stayed put...

I choked on a sob but refused to make a noise. I'd cost Merlin too much already. At least he could escape with his life. He still had his family. Luna, the kittens...

Luna's bright white fur caught my attention as she stalked across the field, closing in on the dueling cats. She didn't have any magic, so what was it she planned to do?

I got my answer in short order when she crept up behind Tom and sank her claws and teeth right into his neck.

Tom flailed against her, but she held tight, impossibly strong. She wasn't only taking his magic, I realized as Tom's slack body fell to the field. All the life had been drained right out of him. Luna had done that.

She'd ended this duel by breaking every rule in the book.

"Luna," I cried, racing toward the cats. "What did you just do?"

"He was losing," she said simply with a shrug.

"But you killed him!" I argued as tears splashed down on my cheeks. So much had happened in such a short span of time, and I was having a hard time processing it all. "Why did you kill him?" I barked out.

"Merlin needs his magic," Luna said coldly, then turned on me with claws extended. She leapt toward me, her eyes red with rage.

I took a step back, but it wasn't enough to escape the oncoming attack.

Luna fell upon me, and everything went black.

17

*T*he next thing I knew I was struggling back to consciousness in a very unfamiliar place.

Standing.

Chained to a boulder.

On top of a mountain.

Oh, boy...

I yanked against my chains, but they had zero give.

Merlin. What had happened to Merlin?

My eyes strained as they scanned the darkness, at last landing upon a small metal cage, not unlike the kind a human would use to trap a skunk or raccoon that had gotten too close to the house.

Merlin lay unconscious inside.

"Merlin! Wake up!" I whisper-yelled. Even though I didn't see anyone else up here with us, our captor could still be nearby. We needed to find a way to escape before it was too late.

"How did we get here?" I asked him, but still he didn't stir. That's when I remembered.

Luna.

She'd killed Tom and then turned on me. But why?

Merlin moaned in his sleep but didn't acknowledge my pleas for help. At least I knew he was alive, even though he wouldn't be helping me make an escape plan any time soon.

I struggled against the chains again, grunting and pulling until I ran out of breath.

"Give it up," a deep and eerie voice commanded from somewhere nearby. "You can't win."

I scanned the summit but couldn't see anyone.

"Who are you? And why have you brought us here?" I shouted into the darkness.

"Pretty demanding for someone who has no options left," the voice said with a cruel chuckle. Well, at least he found this entertaining. I, however, was not amused. I also couldn't place the voice. It was familiar and strange at the same time.

My eyes narrowed in on the sound and finally spotted a black cat perched at the edge of the mountaintop.

Beside the cat, a cauldron flared to life, glowing a hideous swampy green.

"Mr. Fluffikins?" I asked cautiously. But hadn't he departed for his own town with Drake in tow? And wasn't he supposed to be one of the good guys?

The cat spun to face me, backlit by the brewing magic. "Recognize me now?"

The cat's chest was pure black, its eyes a bright glowing green. Mr. Fluffikins had a tiny patch of white on his chest and golden orb eyes. This wasn't him.

But what other black cats did we—? *Oh.*

"Dash," I said through gritted teeth.

"Took you long enough." The dangerous illusion witch simpered at me as if this were all a game. "But then again, I believe you know me better like this."

A poof of magic obscured my view. When it cleared, a no-nonsense police officer scowled back at me. This was the original form in which I'd met Dash, as the cop investigating my old boss Harold's death. Of course, it had all been a trap. As an illusion witch, Dash could take on any form she pleased.

At least I'd always thought of Dash as female since I'd first met the illusion witch under the guise of a police woman. Now, however, I was almost certain the black cat was male. Wait, why was I wasting time trying to figure out pronouns for a cat who almost certainly wanted to kill me?

Think, Gracie. Think!

"Where's Luna?" I demanded as I broke out into a cold sweat.

Another cloud of magic filled my vision, and out stepped a pure white cat with glistening blue eyes.

"I'm right here, dear," Dash said in Luna's voice.

I should have known. Luna would never betray us. It had been Dash the whole time— or at least since we'd entered Nocturna.

I tried to lunge forward, but the chains held me securely in place. "What did you do with her?"

Dash shifted back into her natural form. A plain and unassuming black cat. "I don't see why it matters. You'll never see each other again."

"Tell me where she is!" I yelled, fighting against my chains with renewed fervor.

"Relax. Enjoy your last few hours of life. If it helps settle you down, I can assure you that the white cat is just fine. You on the other hand? You're going to die." Dash let out a dry chuckle. I'd never wanted to smack an animal so badly, not even the zombie squirrels who had tried their best to kill me earlier that day.

Dash looked up and silently studied the night sky full of stars for a moment, then said, "You all could have lived, you know? My plan was simple. Get you to Nocturna to see the blood witch. Take said blood, and none of you would ever be the wiser. I could have carried out this plan with zero casualties. But now because of you, many will die."

I swallowed hard, unsure of how I would

get out of this one, especially without Merlin's aid.

Right now, I needed a miracle.

18

"*L*et me go," I demanded, refusing to die silently—or at all, if I could help it. "Nobody has to get hurt. We can end this all now."

"And why would I do that?" Dash asked, returning to the glowing cauldron and studying the brew.

"Because deep down you're good," I chanced.

Dash laughed bitterly. "Someone has been watching too many fairy tale movies, I think. Because I can assure you I'm bad to the bone."

The notes of that famous old song played in my mind, and I cursed the black cat for adding a catchy ear worm to my current list of problems. I shook my head to regain clarity, focus. Only one thing mattered right now, and that was escaping.

"Why are you doing this?" I asked. "What's in it for you?"

Dash turned a pair of stark green eyes on me. "Oh, that's really quite simple. When I realized what you and Merlin were, the connection you shared, I knew I'd finally found what I'd been waiting centuries for."

"Centuries? Nobody's that old."

"Once again, you are wrong. I am nearly one thousand years old."

I gasped. Hadn't expected that one. "But how?"

Dash smiled, baring sharp white fangs. "You are but an ancestor, the last scion. I, however, am the original."

"You're the imposter Merlin," I said, knowing innately that it was true. It was the only thing that made sense, given how interested she—or, I guess, he—was in Merlin's and my lineage. "But I thought you died."

A puff of magic replaced the little black cat

with a very old man whose white beard stretched to his ankles. "Everyone thought I did. Lucky for me, my illusions kept me hidden until I could find what I needed."

"You were the first familiar. You pledged your loyalty to the real Merlin!" I spat at him, disgusted.

Dash appeared unfazed. "Yes, well, why be the servant when one can be the master?"

This was awful. The only other familiars I'd met had both turned evil in their lust for power. If I survived this, would the same happen to me?

I thought back to the last time we'd faced Dash in a confrontation. If I could keep him talking, it would buy us time. We could still get out of this, Merlin and me.

"Why did you send those zombies after us?" That part still didn't make sense to me.

"Oh, that's easy. Have you really not figured it out yet? I needed to get you to Nocturna. Luckily, you're nothing if not predictable. You came here just as soon as you could get your master to agree, didn't you?"

"Merlin and I are really more of a partnership," I corrected, glancing to my fallen ally in his cage. *Please, please wake up.*

"Does it matter when you'll both die at daybreak?"

"Why do you want to kill us?"

"Why not? By the way, I know what you're doing. You're trying to keep me talking to delay my evil plan. But it doesn't matter. This all has to go down at a very specific time, and I already told you when that is."

"Daybreak," I said through dry lips. "And even you call your own plan *evil*. Shouldn't that tell you something?"

"Good, evil," Dash droned. "They're more alike than you think. The perception of both changes with time. You may consider me evil, but future generations will see me as a god."

"You're a monster," I spat, which took some effort since my mouth was well on its way to going dry.

"And your opinion doesn't matter. You are nothing more than a footnote in the legend of my glory. With your blood connection and the stars in perfect alignment, I will reforge the mighty Excalibur and use it to gain ultimate power over both the magical and the mundane worlds alike."

"You sound like a crazy person," I said.

"You try waiting almost one thousand years for your revenge, and see how you like it."

"Revenge? Against who?"

"Merlin granted me one ultimate wish as his thanks for my taking on the role of his familiar. And when he didn't like it, he tried to trick me out of what was due to me."

"You asked to be as powerful as him," I shouted. I knew Dash's logic made sense in his own mind, but it certainly didn't ring true in mine. "Familiars are only supposed to be vessels."

"Now!" Dash-Merlin-whoever exploded. "Why do you think those rules are in place? Hmm?"

"He cursed you. How did you survive?"

"No, he forced me into hiding. Once the magic was granted, he couldn't take it back. Not without this." He reached two hands into the cauldron and extracted a glittering sword.

"Is that—?" My breath hitched.

"Excalibur. Yes. At least it will be. Nearly one thousand years ago to this day, your ancestor Arthur pulled it from a stone, declaring it the ultimate weapon. But that's not why Excalibur was made, nor what it was meant to do."

I blinked hard. None of what this guy was telling me lined up with what I knew of the original legends. "Come again now?"

"Merlin made it for me. Not because—"

"I'm sorry. This is getting really confusing. We're up to three Merlins now, and it's making it hard for me to follow."

The dark wizard groaned. "Very well. The original cat sorcerer created this weapon, not to take one's life but to take one's magic."

"It was meant for you."

"Yes, but I'd already managed to escape. He became so frustrated that he jammed it into that stone. And by doing that, he couldn't extract it himself."

"Or he would lose his magic," I concluded.

Dash smiled wide. "Precisely."

"So Arthur...?"

"Was a means to an end. Because he pulled the sword from the stone, he would never be able to wield his own magic, even if he wanted to. And that made him the perfect subservient familiar... Oh, look who's finally decided to join us."

My eyes zoomed toward the cage where at last Merlin—my Merlin—was beginning to stir.

19

*M*erlin roused and attempted a standing position, but his back thumped the top of the cage, forcing him back down in a crouch. He shook his head before glancing around the summit.

"Gracie!" he shouted when his eyes landed upon me.

"Merlin, it's okay," I called back, relief flooding my chest. With Merlin's help, we still had a chance. "We're going to get out of this."

"Haven't you been listening to anything I said?" Dash demanded, stomping over to me in a fit.

"Yeah, I heard you. But you lost before, and I'm willing to bet you'll lose again."

"Oh, a bet? What are the stakes? Oh, I know. How about your life." The old wizard chuckled, clearly amused with his own banter.

"Who's this guy?" Merlin asked, his words coming out slurred. The lack of magic still weakened him. We were at a definite disadvantage.

I sighed. "It's a long story, but that's Dash who also happens to be the original imposter Merlin. He's going to kill us so he can reforge Excalibur or something like that."

Dash rounded on me, his gaze filled with venom. "Hey, show a little respect. I worked hard on that plan. And you're leaving all the best parts out."

I shrugged, enjoying the fact that I was getting to him. Right now that was the only way I had to fight back. "It's kind of a convoluted plan, if you ask me. Is that the best you could come up with when you practically had a millennium to do so?"

"It's flawless," he shouted, sending a spray of spittle my way. "Granted, that ridiculous duel set things slightly off course, but the end result will be the same. Many years ago, our ancestors formed an eternal bond when

Arthur pulled Excalibur from the stone. The sword was forged by the cat wizard to rob me of my magic, but instead Arthur was the first person to succumb to its curse, meaning the three of us and our bloodlines were thusly tied for eternity."

I cracked a smile. "Thusly, huh?"

"Enough!" Dash's shout echoed across the distance, proving just how isolated we were on top of this mountain.

"Yes, I think I've heard enough," Merlin ground out, still trapped in an awkward crouch position, thanks to the relatively small size of the cage. "You're the imposter wizard, but I'm the real deal. The last in the most powerful magical line to ever grace this planet. Which means I can beat you, you big fake."

True, he didn't have much room to maneuver in the cage, but that didn't stop Merlin from lightly kicking back his feet in his classic lightning summoner maneuver.

Nothing happened outside the cage.

But inside, Merlin let out a stuttering gasp and fell flat on his stomach.

Dash laughed evilly. "You think I wouldn't lightning-proof that thing? It's a magical cage.

Anything you try to cast will only feed the cage and make it stronger. There's no way out."

Merlin panted as he rose and threw himself at the side of the cage.

Nothing, much to Dash's amusement.

But I refused to accept defeat. Magic couldn't free us, but I'd never had any of my own in the first place. We needed a non-magical solution, and I would find it.

Dash returned Excalibur to the cauldron and continued to work on his potion, doing what I had no idea. My eyes grew heavy as I watched him.

No! If I fell asleep, it would all be over.

"You never told us what you plan to do once you reforge that thing. Other than kill us, I mean."

Dash ignored me.

"Yoo-hoo!" I called. "Earth to Dash, or Merlin, or whoever you are!"

The bearded wizard spun to face me. "I am many people in one. I am everyone, thus no one."

"Uh-huh. So what about the rest of your plan? Don't you want to share it with me?"

"Why? You'll be dead anyway." A small

smile played at his lips. I'm glad the thought of my demise could bring his dark little heart a bit of joy because I would definitely not be the one dying today. Still, I had to play to his vanity to get him to keep talking.

"True, but I'm still curious," I managed.

"Well, it's still a bit early, but I see no reason why we can't get things ready." Dash returned to the cauldron and extracted the sword once more. He carried it over to me, stopping a few feet out of reach. Then returned to his cat form.

This was my chance to fight.

I kicked out but missed by a mile.

He ignored me as he raised a paw and extended his claws, then dragged them across his chest with a gasp of pain. Blood dripped to the ground, splashing onto the sword.

"With our three bloodlines combined, I will reforge Excalibur and use it to seal the portal between Nocturna and the human world, so none can ever rise against me again. And then I will rule as a god, the most powerful—the only —magical being left in the mundane universe. Happy?"

Dash leapt on top of the boulder to which I

was chained and jumped down to my chest, staring me in the eye.

"And now it's your turn to contribute. I'll just be taking some of your blood now."

"Like heck you will!" I raged and writhed but still couldn't free myself.

Dash struck out with a paw and slashed me across the face. I squeezed my eyes shut tight as he made impact, and when I opened them again I found myself someplace entirely different.

20

I stared down at the cash register. It blinked the numbers *$4.15* at me— the price of our thirty-ounce classic pumpkin spice latte, plus tax. In my hand, I clenched a crisp five-dollar bill.

Glancing up, I saw a customer waiting with one hand extended as he used the other to scroll through something on his cell phone.

Right. I must have really spaced out there for a second.

I made the correct change and handed it over. "Your drink will be ready soon," I said with my best customer-facing smile, then walked over to Kelley who had already fired up the espresso machine and gotten to work on the order.

A thick fog crowded the edges of my mind. I hadn't felt like this since I foolishly attempted to down twenty-one shots on my twenty-first birthday. I'd only made it to seven before I barfed all over my date for that night and forever gave up recreational drinking.

I didn't remember drinking last night. In fact, I didn't remember anything about last night at all... Or this morning, either. I just woke up, and I was here at work.

Huh. It seemed I really could do this job while sleeping. Next I'd have to try one hand tied behind my back.

"How has your day been so far?" the next customer asked me with a grin.

I returned her smile and turned back to the cash register. I loved our friendly customers. Increasingly, people treated me like a nuisance, an inconvenient distraction from whatever they were doing on their phones—even though they themselves were the ones who'd chosen to come to the coffee shop.

"It's a good day. Beautiful," I answered, even though I couldn't remember much of it so far.

But no customer—no matter how friendly— wanted to hear the ravings of a mad barista.

Because I was going crazy, right?

Or losing it?

It being my memories.

I took the customer's order and cashed her out. As soon as she left, another came to take her place.

Then another.

And another.

I had no downtime between orders. Granted, Harold's always tended to be busy, but this was ridiculous. I didn't even recognize a single person who came in, and normally we had a steady flow of regulars.

"Kelley?" I asked, walking away from the register and the new customer who stood waiting.

"Hmmm?" she asked as she continued to work the espresso machine.

"Does anything seem off to you today?" I ventured, shifting my weight to one side.

She continued her work without even taking a second to glance up at me, but at least she answered. "Off how?"

I shrugged, wishing I could explain it.

Kelley chuckled. "Looks like someone had a few too many cold ones last night."

I grabbed her arm, but still she didn't look at me. "I don't drink, Kelley. You know that."

"Must have slipped my mind," she said coolly. "Now get back to the register. You have a line."

I followed my boss's orders, even though I now felt more out of sorts than ever. Kelley always made time for small talk, no matter how busy we got. It was important to her to keep up staff morale. And I was one of her best friends. If I came to her because something was wrong, she'd stop everything to help me through it.

"Welcome to Harold's. I'll be right back," I told the customer at the front of the line, then zipped back toward Kelley to test a theory I'd just developed.

"Do you think Drake could be cheating on you?" I asked her. Admittedly, this was a risk. Last time we'd spoken, she'd been intensely worried that Drake's sudden trip away meant he had another woman on the side.

I didn't want to rekindle that worry in my friend, but I also needed to get a stronger response out of Kelley. That would at least ease my own worry, that nagging feeling that something just wasn't right here.

"He wouldn't cheat on me," she said with a dreamy smile. "We're way too happy for him to go and mess things up like that."

Okay, that did it!

Where was I and who was this standing before me? Because it definitely wasn't the Kelley Carmine I knew and loved.

"Sorry, but I've gotta go," I told her, tearing off my apron and dropping it onto the floor.

"You can't just walk away mid-shift!" she shouted.

"Watch me," I called back as I raced around the counter and toward the exit.

21

*B*efore I could make it to the door, a strong hand reached out and grasped my arm.

Drake.

"Hey. Where are you off to in such a hurry?" he asked with his usual chill demeanor, a stark contrast to the sobbing heap he'd become when last we met.

"Something's not right here," I informed him, my voice low to keep the milling herd of customers from overhearing. "I have to go."

"It's weird, right?" came his reply. "One second I was hanging out with Fluffikins and the gang in Beech Grove, and the next I'm here at work."

I took a second to process this. "So you were somewhere else, and then suddenly you ended up here? I think maybe that's what happened to me, too." I racked my brain trying to remember but still came up infuriatingly short.

Drake rocked on his heels. "Yeah, probably, considering this is an illusion."

"A what?" That word sounded familiar, but why?

"An illusion," Drake repeated slowly. "You know, as in, fake. Not real."

"Illusion," I mumbled aloud, tasting the word, meditating on it.

And at last everything came into focus.

Dash!

He'd done this. Illusions were his specialty, and he'd had almost a thousand years to practice this particular skill. He'd captured me and Merlin, taken us to the top of that mountain. He was going to use our blood to do something terrible. He already had some of mine, but I didn't know if he'd gotten to Merlin yet.

I had to get back, just in case there was still time.

"Merlin's in trouble," I told Drake as fear squeezed at my heart. "I have to get to him."

"Okay," he said with a shrug. "See you later, then."

He let go of my arm, and I pushed through the door into the blinding sunlight.

No, it was all white. When the light faded, I realized I was back at the cash register staring at the numbers *$4.15*. By trying to leave, I'd reset the illusion.

I ran to Drake, who seemed to be the only sane person in this place.

"That was trippy," he confided.

"How come you're you when nobody else is?" I demanded, staying close and keeping my voice to a whisper.

"That's a weird thing to ask," he said with wide eyes as if I was blowing his mind right now.

"I'm serious. Kelley isn't herself. She's acting weird, but you're the same as always. Why?"

Drake tilted his head as he thought about this. "Now that I think about it, I'm not really me."

I pursed my lips, not knowing how to respond to that.

Luckily, he continued on. "Like my mind is here, but my body isn't."

"Drake, I'm looking at you right now. You. Your body."

He shook his head. "No, I don't think so. Watch."

I stared at him, but nothing happened except that he fell silent for a few moments.

"See," he exclaimed after about a minute.

"See what?" To my eye, not a thing had happened, but Drake appeared giddy.

"I left," he enthused as if I were supposed to not only take this all in stride but also be duly impressed. "I went back to Beech Grove and said *what up* to Mr. Fluffikins."

"Drake, you didn't go anywhere. You were here the whole time," I argued as the beginnings of a headache pressed at my temples.

He touched his chest and frowned. "Not me. This isn't the real me. Well, this body isn't. The inside me is here with you, but the outside me is back with Fluffikins."

"Drake, listen to me," I said pulling him toward the wall so we had a bit of privacy.

"Right now I'm battling a really strong illusion witch. He sent me here as a distraction because I was asking too many questions or something. But I have to get back."

Drake nodded along. He was *laissez faire* about everything, but at least he wasn't stupid. I clung to that now.

"How did you leave just now?"

He twisted his hands in front of him. "I don't know. I just did it."

I groaned. So not helpful. "But how? I need to leave now. Can you teach me?"

He thought about this for a second before speaking again. "I just opened my eyes, my real eyes, and then I was in Beech Grove. When I closed them again, I was here. I don't really know how else to explain it."

"Okay," I said, licking my lips. "I'm going to try that."

I closed my eyes and tried to picture the summit I'd left behind. When I opened them again, I found Drake watching me in anticipation.

"Did it work?" he asked with a curious expression.

"No. Let me try again." And I did. I tried at

least half a dozen times with increasing frustration, but I couldn't get it to work.

"Drake, I'm stuck," I whined in frustration.

He thrust one hand into his pocket and brought the other up to grope at his opposite arm. "Sorry."

"I'm stuck..." I said again, realizing something. "But you're not. You can help me!"

"Sure. What do you need?"

"Okay, listen up, because this is very important. I need you to go back to Mr. Fluffikins and tell him that an evil wizard has captured me and Merlin and taken us to the top of a very tall mountain in Nocturna. I'm trapped in an illusion, and Merlin is in a magical cage. We have no way out, and the wizard is going to use our blood to cast a very bad, super evil spell. I need you guys to come and save us."

His eyebrows rose one after the other. Finally I had piqued his curiosity "Nocturna? I've never heard of that place before."

"Yeah, but I'm hoping Mr. Fluffikins has. Can you do this, Drake? Can you save the world?"

"Sure, I don't see why not." And then he

was gone, leaving behind the lifeless shell of his illusion.

All I could do now was wait and hope that I had put my trust in the right man—er, vampire —for the job.

22

I blinked my eyes open with a start. The brightly lit coffee shop had transformed into a dark and barren nightscape. I couldn't see anything, save for the glowing light of the stars and moon that hung heavy in the sky above.

One more thing glowed, too—a cauldron filled with rolling bright green liquid.

I was back at the summit!

But how?

A swirl of pink caught my eye, then another surge of green.

Two black cats tumbled in a tangle of magic, Fluffikins versus Dash, good versus evil.

"Drake?" I shouted into the darkness.

"I'm here," he said, level-headed as he stood dangerously close to the edge of the mountaintop.

"You found us!" I was so happy I could cry.

"Took a few tries, but we got here. There are a lot of mountains in this place."

Now I really was crying. Perhaps I wouldn't die today, after all.

"Do you know you're chained to a rock?" Drake asked as the cats continued to fight tooth and nail.

"Yep. Can you free me?" I asked hopefully, struggling against my bonds to show him I was incapable of releasing them myself.

Drake started toward me with a steady stride, focused but not hurried, as if he had all the time in the world.

I tried not to groan, sigh, or roll my eyes. I knew he was capable of emotion. I'd seen it when Mr. Fluffikins had revealed that Drake was secretly a vampire. Did our current situation really not even warrant a bit of pep in his step?

Drake had cleared more than half of the distance between us when all of a sudden his eyes grew wide, and he slumped forward onto the ground.

Dash stood behind him, assessing the damage with obvious pride.

"Drake!" I screamed. "Get up!"

"That should keep him out for the count," the evil wizard said just before Fluffikins hurled into him like a blazing comet, and the cat fight resumed.

I watched them for a while, but it was impossible to tell who was who in this night-time battle of magical black cats. The only saving grace was that their magic sparked in different colors. I wondered why Merlin's matched Dash's green and not Fluffikins's pink.

"Merlin?" I cried out, remembering my cat was still here somewhere, too. "Merlin, are you okay?"

"I'm okay," he said, sounding groggy. "But I still can't escape."

"Did Dash take any of your blood yet?"

"N-no, I don't think so."

"Then we're not too late." We could still do this. And now that the infantry had arrived, we would do this.

"The sun will rise soon. We don't have much time," Merlin warned.

"As long as we can keep Dash from getting your blood, we'll be okay," I promised, hoping that it was one I'd be able to keep.

The two black cats hissed and growled as they rolled about the mountaintop, locked in their magical battle. Dash was much stronger than either me or Merlin, but Mr. Fluffikins could easily hold his own.

My eyes darted from them to Merlin to Drake, waiting for the perfect opportunity to present itself. Somehow or another, we would win. We had to.

The cats tumbled into Dash's glowing cauldron, knocking it over. The swampy liquid sloshed out and seeped into the ground.

"You're too late," Dash boomed in that strange deep voice of his. "The sun is upon us. I just need one last ingredient and Excalibur shall be reborn."

Sure enough, the sun now peeked over the horizon. I'd never been so unhappy to see the dawn of a new day, but now, if we survived this, I would always view the sunrise differently. As a possible end rather than a promising beginning.

Fluffikins glanced up toward the sun. Only for an instant, but it was enough.

As soon as his opponent was distracted, Dash charged for Merlin's cage, ready to steal his blood and bring the cursed artifact back to life.

"No!" I screamed.

But Dash was already at the cage, fiddling with the lock. Although he kept his black cat form, he bespelled one of his claws into a key that fit the lock in question perfectly, no doubt.

Merlin pressed himself against the back wall, trying to put as much distance between himself and the dark wizard as possible.

From the corner of my eyes, a blinding shot of pink streaked across the summit and slammed into Dash like a speeding freight train. It didn't stop with impact, but kept pushing, charging straight off the mountaintop and out into the pre-dawn sky.

The ball of pink magic curved, reversing course and whipping back toward us. It stopped at Drake's side, and the magic faded to nothingness.

"What happened?" I asked Mr. Fluffikins.

"He wasn't paying attention, so I pushed him off the mountain," the big boss cat said, his chest puffed with pride.

"And you are so going to regret that," the dark wizard's voice boomed as he crested over the mountain. But he wasn't a cat anymore, nor was he a hoary-bearded human.

An enormous dragon now treaded air before us.

And he did not look happy.

23

I stared at the monstrous green dragon with my mouth hanging wide open. I'd witnessed a lot of magic in the past few months, but none of it had shaken me quite like the sight of the awful behemoth flapping its wings before me now.

Dragon Dash roared and unleashed a torrent of flames that charred the grass at my feet.

"What's happening?" Drake shouted, finally waking up and scrambling to his feet. "Whoa, cool special effects."

The dragon puked flames and sent them weaving toward Drake.

"No!" I screamed just as the inferno enveloped my poor friend.

The dragon laughed and moved on to his next victim: Mr. Fluffikins.

I stared at the pillar of fire, still burning bright several paces away. Sweat beaded at my brow and above my lip. There's no way Drake could have survived that.

And it was my fault. I'd brought him into this.

In the distance, the cats resumed their battle. Although Dash's new form greatly outweighed the little black cat, Fluffikins did not back down from the battle. He launched himself straight at the menace and picked up the fight exactly where they had left off.

I left the cats to it and hung my head in remembrance as the fire burned itself out.

"Ouch, that was hot," Drake murmured, and when I glanced up I saw him stepping away from a scorched mound of earth. He didn't have a single burn on him. Not even a smudge of soot.

"Drake," I whisper-yelled, when I was sure the two witchy cats were fixated on each other and not paying attention to us.

When he looked my way, I nudged my chin to the side to motion for him to come closer.

"Aren't my new vampire powers awesome?" he asked with an enormous smile. "I literally just walked through fire."

"Yeah, super great." Of course, I had a billion questions to ask about that, but something told me Drake didn't have any of the answers, either. Besides, we had more important things to focus on right now.

"*L*isten," I continued. "I need you to get Merlin out of that cage. Dash unlocked it before Fluffikins pushed him off the edge of the mountain, so you should just have to unlatch it. Okay?"

"Okay."

"And move slowly and quietly. Dash doesn't think you're a threat, and the last thing we want to do is change his mind about that."

Drake gave me the thumbs up, then crept across the summit to Merlin's cage several yards away. Sure enough, he was able to simply unlatch Merlin's cage, no fancy lock fiddling required.

I expected Merlin to jump out of the cage with magic blazing, but instead he crept out with a faltering gait. The poor guy had been through a lot in the last twenty-four hours, and I wasn't sure how much more he could take.

I wanted to shout encouragements at him, but that would risk revealing his new freedom to Dash. For now, I just had to trust that my cat knew what he was doing.

And he was definitely doing something.

Merlin moved slowly but decisively toward me. Was he coming to break my chains? Would I finally be able to join this fight rather than just cheerleading from the sidelines?

No. The Maine Coon stopped a few feet shy of me and my boulder, and I realized in horror what he planned to do.

"Merlin, you can't," I rasped, barely above a whisper. I still couldn't risk alerting Dash to his freedom.

Merlin glanced up and met my eyes for a brief moment before returning his attention to the discarded sword. "We have no other options left," he said stoically.

And before I could stop him, he raised one clawed fist into the air and brought it down hard, swiping against his chest, exactly the same as Dash had done before.

His blood spread across his long fur, then at last dripped down onto the sword.

My cat had just reforged Excalibur, the weapon meant to destroy us.

24

*N*ow infused with the blood of the final member of our cursed trio, the ancient sword glowed a hot and angry white.

Merlin took a deep breath and pulled himself up onto his hindquarters, then pounced down on the sword with both of his front paws.

The sword hissed and sizzled, extending its glow to Merlin's body as well. Together, they shone like a beacon, drawing the dragon's attention straight to them.

"No!" Dash pulled away from Fluffikins and sped toward the light.

"Drake," I yelled, motioning for him to join me again.

"I have a plan," I said as the dragon frantically tried to separate Merlin from the sword, but it seemed as if the two had now fused into one.

I whispered my plan to Drake, but he met me with a grimace of uncertainty. "I don't know. That seems pretty crazy."

"Just trust me on this one. It's our best shot."

He nodded and sauntered away.

"What have you done?" Dash bellowed, though he didn't seem to be asking anyone in particular.

Finally the sword released its hold on Merlin, and my cat fell to his side, completely spent.

The dragon grappled for the sword and easily gained hold. No one was left to fight him for it. With renewed confidence, Dash lunged at Fluffikins, slicing with enormous strength.

"Look out!" Drake and I both screamed.

Mr. Fluffikins produced a pink whip of magic and grabbed onto the sword, easily breaking it free of the dragon's grasp. He then used his magical whip to point the sword at the dragon's heart.

And as his magic held onto Excalibur, it became abundantly clear that the sword hadn't fulfilled its intended purpose. Mr. Fluffikins's magic still burned strong and sparkled bright.

"You idiots have ruined my beautiful plan," the dragon cried when he, too, realized the artifact had failed to rob the other cat of his magic. "For this, you will die!"

Dash and Fluffikins continued their battle, both still equipped with their full abilities. Excalibur fell to the ground, little more than a useless relic now.

Merlin cracked an eye open as he lay panting on the earth.

Drake crouched in the distance, waiting for the perfect moment to act on our plan.

I remained chained to that danged boulder.

"What did you do, you silly cat?" I asked Merlin. Once again tears streamed down my cheeks. I was really turning into quite the crybaby.

"My blood," he said with a shudder. "It's no longer magic. The spell is broken."

"You reforged the artifact and then nullified it so no one else could use it," I realized aloud.

"Yes," he said before passing out again.

"Merlin!" I screamed, but nothing I said or did could wake him.

Please don't be dead; please don't be dead.

It couldn't end like this. We couldn't win this battle only to lose the war. Merlin couldn't die. And he hadn't. I refused to accept it.

Fluffikins and Dash continued to fight for what felt like ages. It must have felt like a long time to Drake, too, because he decided to depart from the original plan.

"Yo, dragon breath!" he shouted, jumping up and waving his hands in the air.

"You! I thought I already disposed of you!" Dash roared and pulled away from Fluffikins, making a beeline for Drake.

Oh, that stupid jerk. Now he was going to die, too. Why couldn't he have just waited like I told him?

I was still weighing this question in my mind when Drake disappeared right before my eyes and reappeared on the dragon's back, driving him on toward the magical cage that had imprisoned Merlin earlier.

At the last possible second, Drake disappeared again. No, that wasn't it. He moved so fast, he became invisible to my human eye.

He leapt from the dragon's back right before the massive monster crashed into that tiny cage.

Being a magic cage, the second the dragon made impact, his power was absorbed into its bars, returning Dash to his natural form.

The old man with the long beard.

First Merlin's magic and now Dash's had made the cage even more powerful, and it easily quadrupled in size to accommodate its new humanoid cargo.

"Lock it!" I screamed, but Drake was already on it.

Fluffikins flew over and landed on the ground with a heavy thump. "It seems your first lesson with Connie went well."

"Yeah, turns out being a vampire isn't so bad," Drake admitted, jamming his hands into the pockets of his jeans.

"All right, you're coming with me," Mr. Fluffikins said to the pitiful creature in the cage before summoning a thick pink mist and flashing them both out of existence.

That just left me, Drake, and Merlin.

"Let me help you with those," Drake said. He zipped over to my side with impossible speed, then grabbed hold of my chains and pulled them apart like they were nothing more than the finest of threads.

I balked. "Could you have done that the whole time?"

"Probably," he admitted. "But I'm still getting the hang of things."

I gave him a high five, then fell to the ground at my cat's side. I scooped Merlin into my arms, and he nestled into my chest. He was still alive but would be mighty embarrassed about this later.

"We have to get back to town and find Luna," I told Drake.

"Let's get going, then," he returned.

"Wait," I said, staring into Merlin's little kitty face. His tongue stuck out slightly between his lips. He looked so innocent in that moment.

"I can't go with you," I said with a sad smile. "I can't leave Nocturna. Not anymore."

25

"*I*f you're not leaving, then I'm not leaving," Drake insisted, totally catching me by surprise.

"I'll be fine," I said, flapping my hand. "Go, if you can."

He kicked at the burnt earth. "Okay, but how?"

"Well, how did you and Mr. Fluffikins get here in the first place?" Honestly, I'd been wondering about that for a while now.

"That pink magic stuff of his," Drake answered without missing a beat.

"I'm sure he'll come back for you once he's done making sure Dash is nice and cozy in that prison he mentioned."

Drake nodded as if it didn't matter. "But what about you?"

I sighed and stared down at the unconscious cat in my arms. "Only Merlin could take me in and out of Nocturna. I'm bound to him as his familiar."

"But he doesn't have magic anymore, right?"

"Right."

Drake's face wore a mix of emotions, so different than his usual tranquility. "So how are you going to get out of here?"

I shivered and hugged Merlin tighter to my chest, suddenly realizing how cold it had become now that the adrenaline had worn off. "I'm not."

He scrunched his nose as if in disgust, then shook his head. "Well, you can't stay on this mountaintop. Let me take you somewhere."

"No, Drake. Really, that's o—"

But before I could finish my argument, he snatched me into his arms and took off down the mountain at a blinding speed. I clung to Merlin as best I could, terrified of dropping him to his death.

"This a good place," Drake said, setting me to my feet a short while later.

I kept my eyes squeezed tight, afraid to look. At least it seemed like the world had stopped spinning around me.

After drawing in a deep, calming breath, I cracked one eye open and stumbled.

Drake reached out a steadying hand, holding me as I held Merlin, who was still out cold.

"You brought me back to the village," I said, surveying the miniaturized Bavarian town that rose up around me.

Drake shrugged. "Seemed as good a place as any."

We both glanced around the quaint village. An old Himalayan couple strolled past us on the other side of the street, but otherwise the place was deserted.

"Excuse me," I called out. "Might I ask a favor?"

They paused and stared at me with huge, unblinking eyes.

"Could you help my friends get back to the other side?"

"Yes, we can help," the lady cat answered

with a cute, squeaky voice. "Our house is just down the road. Meet us back here about ten minutes before dusk, and we'll ready our portal."

"Thank you," I said, dipping my head in a bow. Unfortunately, I'd just realized my mistake.

The Himalayan couple returned my bow and carried on their way.

"They'll get you out of here, but not until later. The portals only open at night," I confided in Drake. Well, at least I'd have company as I figured out this new life of mine.

We both glared up at the sun, which had reached the top of the sky.

Drake offered me a cautious smile. "Well, I can think of worse ways to spend the day, especially since I'm going to have so many of them in my long, immortal life."

"Are you really immortal?" I asked as we navigated the empty walkways of Nocturna. Its feline residents had ambled off to bed by now, it seemed.

"There are still ways I can die. But not many. Most vampires stick around a very long time." He pushed both hands in his pockets and let out a deep, stuttering breath.

"How do you feel about it? Being a vampire, I mean?"

He shrugged. "At first it was a shock, but I'm used to it now."

"Already? I mean, you only found out yesterday."

"Yeah, but I guess I've been one for a couple years now. Remember how I told you about that time I saw the white ghost in the rainstorm?"

I nodded, engrossed in his story.

"I think it happened that night. Fluffikins and his team are trying to help me retrieve that memory. They think it's the key to finding out why I'm different." He frowned for a moment, then rearranged his features into his signature mask of apathy.

"You've always been different, Drake," I pointed out with a laugh.

He chuckled, too, but I could tell his heart wasn't in it. "Yeah, but they mean something else. I can do things vampires aren't supposed to do."

"Like walk through fire?" I suggested.

"That, and other things." He shrugged again. "I dunno. There's a lot for me to figure out."

I wanted to help my friend, but I didn't know how. All I could do was listen while he was in Nocturna and hope for the best after he left it. It would take some getting used to—the idea that all my friends and family would have to carry on their lives without me. They wouldn't even know what had happened...

My phone buzzed in my pocket with an incoming call.

"Really? I have cell service in another dimension?" I fished it out of my pocket and saw that Kelley was the one calling.

"I've gotta take this," I said to Drake before pushing the button to accept her call. "Hello?"

26

"Gracie!" Kelley shouted into my ear via the cell phone. "You'll never guess what!"

I put her on speaker so Drake could hear, too, but lifted a finger to my mouth so he would keep quiet. The last thing Kelley needed was to find out that Drake and I were together in the wee hours of the morning. It was all innocent enough, but there was zero percent of the truth I could readily share with her, and I was far too exhausted to create a compelling lie.

"What?" I asked, adding as much cheer to my voice as I could muster.

"Well, I had a hard time sleeping last night

because I was worried about me and Drake," she began.

When she paused to take a breath, I rushed to Drake's defense. "Kelley, I already told you. You two are—"

"No, listen. That's not important. I mean, it is, but that's not why I'm calling." She took a hurried breath and jumped right back in. "I couldn't get to sleep, so I went outside for a little fresh air. And I think I found your cat."

I glanced down at Merlin, still cradled in the crook of one arm as I held onto the cell phone with my other. "Really, because he's right here with me."

"Yeah, but you have two cats, right? The big fluffy brown one and the smaller white one."

I gasped. "Did you find Luna?"

"I'm pretty sure I did. Hang on, I'll text you a picture."

My phone chimed, and I swiped up to open the text message. Sure enough, Luna's bright blue eyes beamed back at me.

"It's not a good one, but it's the best I can do," she said as I studied the image.

"Is Luna okay?" I pleaded. "Is she with you now?"

Kelley yawned as if to prove her story about missing out on sleep last night. Well, she wasn't the only one.

"I've been trying to call all night," she said, fatigue still evident in her voice, "but I only just now could get through. Where have you been?"

On top of a mountain fighting a dragon, among other things.

"Um, that's not important," I said. "Is Luna okay?"

"Yeah, I mean, I think so. She's stuck at the bottom of my well, so I'm not one-hundred percent sure, but she's been meowing up a storm. That's how I found her in the first place."

I could just picture Kelley standing over the well and glancing down at Luna as we spoke. Thank goodness, she had found her. Merlin would be so relieved when he woke up.

"Oh my gosh, Kelley, you have to get her out of there," I shouted, drawing a strange look from a wiry calico as she trotted by.

"I already called the fire station," my friend assured me. "They help cats out of trees, so why not wells? They said they'll stop by when they have a free moment to help. So I'm just hanging around waiting. Luckily, I planned to take the day off anyway. Hey, so when are you coming over?"

I lowered the phone and gulped back a fresh wave of nausea. What could I say? I couldn't come to her house now or ever again. I was stuck in Nocturna forever but had no way of explaining that to her.

"I'll be there as soon as I can," I managed to choke out before ending the call.

"Luuuunaaaa," Merlin moaned and turned over in my arms.

"She's safe. Kelley found her," I told him with a huge smile. I was so happy that the little cat family would be okay, even if I wouldn't be part of it anymore.

"We have to get back," Merlin insisted, tapping me with a paw. "Put me down. I have to go to Luna."

"But it's already morning, and we're stuck in Nocturna until at least tonight," I informed him, but set him on his feet, anyway. I was glad he'd regained his full consciousness. That was one less thing to worry about in this very worrisome day.

"Hey, that thing works, right?" Drake

pointed to my phone. He used his other hand to extract his phone from his pocket and glance at the screen.

"No bars," he informed me, waving it before me. "Remind me to switch to your carrier when we're out of here." He held out his hand, open-palmed. "May I?"

"Uh, sure." I placed the cell phone in his waiting hand and watched as he copied a number from his phone into mine.

"Shh, it's ringing!"

Someone picked up on the other end of the line. I could just barely hear a muffled hello.

Drake's face lit up like a bonfire. "Tawny, hey. Put Fluffikins on."

27

"*Um*, could you put somebody else on evil-wizard babysitting duty and come get us, please," Drake said once Fluffikins had answered and he'd switched the call over to speaker phone.

"Where are you?" the black cat demanded in that creepy snake-like voice of his.

Drake blinked up at the sky and then looked around, presumably searching for landmarks. "That city. Nocturna. Right near the town square. There's a fountain."

"But Drake," I started to argue. "The portal only opens at—"

I stopped talking when Mr. Fluffikins

appeared standing a few feet before us in his famous pink burst of magic.

Drake ended the call and handed my phone back to me.

Meanwhile, my jaw practically fell to my chest. "I don't understand. How?"

"Your cats' magic and mine are different," Fluffikins explained like the answer should have been obvious. "The same rules don't apply."

"Is that why their magic is green and yours is pink?" I asked, still dumbfounded.

"Something like that." The black cat plopped his rear onto the cobblestone walkway and flicked his tail thoughtfully. "I'll admit, I haven't quite figured out how so many magical systems can exist in the same space without following the same rules. But I assure you I won't rest until I figure it out."

"Are there more out there? Besides yours and what I had?" Merlin asked, settling himself at my feet.

"Yes. Yours originated in England some thousand years ago. Mine is much older than that, as old as the Earth itself, if not more." A smile stretched from one whiskered cheek to the next. Mr. Fluffikins clearly took pride in the seniority of his magic system.

"What else is out there?" I asked, crouching down to run my fingers through Merlin's thick fur.

"I don't know, but I intend to find out. Once I've finished training my replacement—"

"Tawny," Drake provided with an enormous sappy grin. Someone definitely had a crush. Not good news for Kelley, but then again, she and Drake probably wouldn't last much longer, given his new creature of the night status.

"Yes. Once Tawny takes over my post as diplomat for the Peach Plains region, I intend to travel the world and learn all I can about the various magic systems out there and how they fit together."

"Does that mean you can get Gracie out of here?" Merlin asked. It was only now that I realized his previously green eyes had settled into a honey brown. The magic inside him had died, and by his own paw.

"I can try," Fluffikins responded with a nod.

"Everyone stand close and place a hand on me."

We scrambled over to him and did as instructed.

A pink mist swirled around us, then dissipated, leaving me all by myself on that cobblestone street.

A few seconds later, Mr. Fluffikins returned.

"I'm sorry, Gracie," he said. "It seems you are tied to the Nocturna system of magic and thus bound to its rules."

Tears threatened to fall, but I forced them back. "I understand."

"They can still visit you here," he offered, blinking up at me.

I nodded sadly. "I know."

"And I will search for an answer in my research, a way to bring you back to the mundane world."

"Thank you," I murmured.

Mr. Fluffikins shot me one last doleful look, then vanished for good this time.

Alone again, the full weight of my exhaustion settled over me. I hadn't slept at all last night. Instead, I'd been embroiled in one deadly battle after the next.

I was so, so tired.

And so I lay down, right there on the street, and closed my eyes. It didn't take long for me to drift off into a world all my own.

28

I woke up to a soft pair of paws kneading into my side.

"Merlin?" I mumbled. "Luna?"

But when I opened my eyes, I saw the elderly Himalayan female sitting at my side wearing a concerned expression.

"Do you still want to use our portal?" she asked as she continued to paw at me.

"I'm fine, thank you." I sat up and rubbed the sleep from my eyes.

"Are you all right, dear? You look pretty run-down."

Dear. That was Luna's pet name for me. If I closed my eyes again, I could almost imagine that she and Merlin were right here with me. But no, I was all on my own.

Forever.

I broke into a giant racking sob and let loose a pained wail.

"Let's find you something to warm your belly. Come with me," the kind stranger said, and I let her guide mc toward her home.

"I don't think you'll fit comfortably inside, but please wait here and I will bring you a bit of milk," she said before running into her small, thatched cottage.

I waited, my tummy rumbling at the thought of obtaining nourishment. I'd been too scared, sad, tired, what-have-you to notice my hunger until now.

I tried to focus on my surroundings rather than the deep hunger in my belly.

Nearby, the village began to rouse. Nightfall was fast approaching, which meant it was time for them to start their day. And I watched as cats of all colors and stripes exited their homes and set out on journeys to places unknown.

A litter of black and white patched kittens followed after their mother in a little line, moving their paws quickly in an effort to keep up.

I smiled to myself. My world had ended, but all around me life went on. There were still happy endings and new beginnings. And I could make them happen for myself as long as I didn't give up.

I spied a brown fluffy cat racing up and down the pavement with an all-white kitten clutched in its mouth. As the pair drew closer, I realized that the baby couldn't have been more than a few days old. Its eyes hadn't even opened yet.

Oh, gosh. I hoped everything was okay.

I stood and moved toward the Himalayan couple's front door, knocking gently. "Excuse me, ma'am. I think there might be some trouble."

She hissed in fright, then peered at me through the window. "What trouble did you bring to my door?" she asked with wide eyes.

"I didn't mean to. I mean, I don't think, I—"

"Cat got your tongue," Merlin said from behind me. His voice came out muffled, but I would recognize it anywhere.

I spun to face him, and there he stood. He

was the brown fluff ball racing through the streets with that white kitten in his mouth.

"Is that...?" My voice cracked, and I began to cry.

Yes, again.

"Here. Take him," Merlin said through a mouthful of fur.

I stretched my palms forward and allowed him to lay the tiny kitten onto my hands, then stood, lifting him to my face.

"So tiny!" I squealed.

"What's his name?" I asked with the biggest smile ever lighting my face.

Merlin raised his head high and sniffed at the night sky. "He doesn't have one yet. Luna and I had something more pressing to take care of first."

"Luna! Is she okay?"

"Yes, she's no worse for the wear. Came through the birth like a champ to deliver four healthy babes. Three girls and this boy."

"Oh!" I cried again between peppering light kisses to the tiny fluffer-nutter in my hands. "Thank you for bringing him to see me."

"I didn't bring him to see you," Merlin

corrected, his face lightening into a smile. "I brought him to take you home."

I straightened with a start. "What?"

"My genius wifey pointed something out to me after I returned."

"Yeah, and what was that?"

"You're tied to my blood."

"Yes, and you're no longer magical, which is why I'm stuck here."

"I'm not, but I'm no longer the only one with my blood."

I stared down at the baby in my hands. "You don't mean."

"He got me here," Merlin pointed out. "Now let's see if he can get you back home. We need you there, Gracie. You're one of us."

Cue a whole lake of tears from Ms. Gracie Springs. At the end of the day, it seemed my last name fit me like a glove.

"Thank you for helping me, but I'm going now," I called to the peeping seal-point Himalayan before crouching back down to meet Merlin head-on.

"Let's go home," I said, holding the kitten in one hand while petting him with the other.

"Finally. I thought you'd never ask."

29

*E*verything back home was exactly as I'd left it the night before. Everything except the addition of four squirming newborn kittens.

"I just love them. Every single one of them," I gushed to Luna as she introduced me to each of the three girls. They all looked just like their father, while the sole boy took after his mother.

"You'll have to help us figure out what to call them. Merlin and I can't agree on a single name," she said, helping the smallest of the three girls latch on for feeding time.

"I'd be happy to."

Virginia chose that precise moment to pop out of the wall and shout, "Boo!"

The kittens shrieked and burrowed into Luna for safety.

"You did not just scare my cat nieces and nephews!" I bit out, seething with a rage like I'd never felt before.

Virginia cackled. "I'm going to like having the bitty brats around, I think."

"It was you!" I snapped, carefully pushing myself to my feet and charging at the ghost.

"I have no idea what you're talking about," she said, already growing bored with me apparently, as she floated back toward the wall.

But I refused to let her off that easily. "You were spying on us for weeks. You told Dash when he could get a clear shot at Luna to make the switch. I'm guessing you also told him where he could hide her. Or was it just a coincidence that she ended up at the bottom of Kelley's well?"

"My well. My house!" Virginia corrected. "And what does it matter? Somehow you fools still managed to win in the end, so who cares about what part I had in things?"

"I care," I said, jabbing my thumb toward my chest. "Especially since you're spooking the babies."

"Oh, boo hoo." Virginia laughed uproariously at her own joke.

I reached into my pocket and took out my cell phone.

"What are you doing?" Virginia asked, fright creeping into her voice.

"Calling the exterminator," I said with a deliciously wicked grin.

Drake answered after the second ring. "Yellow."

"Hi, Drake. Are you with Mr. Fluffikins?" I asked breathlessly.

"Yup."

"I need a favor." I quickly explained our problem.

"Yeah, we can help with that," Drake said before hanging up.

About five minutes later, Drake, Mr. Fluffikins, and an old man with a long white beard popped into my living room.

I screamed and stretched out my arms to form a protective barricade for Luna and the kittens. "Dash is right behind you!" I yelled in warning.

Drake stared at me, his brow scrunched

with confusion. "What? Oh, that's not Dash. This is—"

Virginia let out a terrible wail, drowning out Drake's words.

I glanced over just in time to see the Dash doppelgänger swish a massive scythe and suck Virginia's disembodied spirit into the blade.

"What just happened?" I asked, equal parts thrilled and terrified.

Drake waggled his eyebrows. "You had a soul to reap, so I brought my reaper friend."

The old guy in the suit bowed, then went to check out the contents of my fridge.

"Thank you," I called after him.

He simply lifted a hand in acknowledgment and returned to foraging about my refrigerator.

"He doesn't talk much," Drake said with a shrug.

"C'mon, you two. I want you to meet the kittens," I said, grabbing Drake's hand and pulling him after me.

Mr. Fluffikins followed us to the far corner of my bedroom where Luna had arranged a pile of blankets and old clothes to create a nest for her and the kittens.

Merlin joined us, too, having returned from whatever he was doing outside. He didn't say, and I didn't ask.

"They're so tiny," Drake crooned as he settled himself cross-legged on the floor.

"You should have seen them a few hours ago," I said, every bit the proud aunt. "I swear, they've at least doubled in size since then."

We all sat and waited for the kittens to finish their meal.

The little boy was the first to pull away from Luna. He wiggled his paws against the floor and scooted away from his mother's belly. Being that the kittens were still incredibly young—still less than a day old at this point— they never strayed far from Luna.

Right now, however, the little tike was moving determinedly across the room. I'd never seen any of the babies venture so far from their mother. But, I'll be darned, that white kitten kept going until he bumped into Drake's foot, then he stopped and mewled.

Drake laughed and scooped the baby into his hands.

"Whoa," he said, after lifting the baby to his face. "How come it has red eyes?"

I chuckled. "Don't be silly, Drake. They won't open their eyes for another week at least."

He slowly turned the little boy around so I could see his face. Sure enough, his eyes had popped open and were now glowing a bright and angry red.

"Well, this isn't good," Fluffikins said.

30

For the next week, Drake and Mr. Fluffikins visited every day. They said they just wanted to see how we were getting on after the big showdown with Dash, but it was quite obvious that they were actually observing the little white kitty with red eyes.

None of his sisters had opened their eyes yet, and they still mostly scooted and paddled to move from place to place. Our boy, however, was now able to run, scamper, and pounce. His favorite activity was playing with the laser pointers I'd picked up at the local pet store. Strangely, he was able to catch the dot each and every time we played, frying the battery on the laser pointer and effectively running our game.

Then there was that one time he sneezed and summoned a tiny tornado right in the house!

When he started biting Luna during nursing time so that her milk mixed with blood, Merlin and I knew we had to do something fast.

That day when the Beech Grove crew showed up for their visit, we left Drake with Luna and the babies while Merlin and I pulled Mr. Fluffikins outside for an important discussion.

"What's wrong with my son?" Merlin asked.

"He's a vampire," Fluffikins stated plainly.

"He's a witch," Merlin countered, kicking up his back feet in anger. He could no longer summon lightning—or anything else for that matter—but he still retained some of his magical mannerisms.

"Actually, I think he's both," I offered in quick order. Both cats turned to me. "I think something happened with Drake the first day they met. They bonded."

"And now Drake is his familiar?" Merlin asked, aghast.

"I'm not sure which is witch," I said, chuckling at my pun.

The cats, however, didn't even crack half a smile between them.

"That day when you came to take Drake," Merlin said, dancing on his front paws. "You said that vampires don't drink blood anymore. That it's an outdated practice. Then why is my boy doing it?"

Mr. Fluffikins cleared his throat before saying, "Human vampires don't."

"What about cat vampires?"

Mr. Fluffikins shook his head and sighed. "I don't know. There's never been one before."

We all drew quiet at this revelation.

"Will he be okay?" I asked at last.

The black cat nodded. "He's very strong and developing at an accelerated rate. Surely, you have noticed that."

Merlin and I both nodded, too.

"As hard as this is to hear, you need to let him go. Let him leave with Drake. They need to be together."

Merlin's eyes searched the horizon. "But how will I know he's okay?" he squeaked.

Fluffikins reached forward and set a paw on top of Merlin's "You have my word. I'll treat them both as if they are my own."

My cat turned to me. "Luna won't like this."

"I know," I said with a sad smile. "I don't like it either. But I understand."

"Me, too. But let me talk to her alone," he said, and then without waiting ran back through the cat flap.

A few moments later, Drake came out to join us in the front yard.

"I heard you broke up with Kelley," I said conversationally, because it felt like a lighter topic than the whole vampire thing. She'd called me a few days back and cried her eyes out as we both dug into cartons of ice cream and streamed a sappy chick flick together on Netflix.

"It was the right thing to do," he said. "Please promise me you'll find a good guy for her, someone who deserves her."

"Of course, I will!" I practically shouted. So much had changed in the last week, but Kelley was still one of my best friends. That would never change.

"I'm moving," Drake added softly. "Not Beech Grove, but somewhere new."

"There was an opening for town vampire," Mr. Fluffikins explained. "I vouched for him."

"Well, congratulations. I'm sure you and your kitten will love it there." I was too consumed with sadness over the departing kitten to offer him a smile now.

Drake looked to Fluffikins, confusion evident in his expression.

"You two share an unbreakable bond. Much like Gracie and Merlin," the cat boss reasoned.

It was true. Even after Merlin sacrificed his magic, I still remained tied to him and his family. Now anyone who saw Drake and the kitten together knew they belonged together.

"Well, at least I know I'll have a friend where I'm going."

"What will you name him?" I asked, hating that the kittens were more than a week old and still didn't have names.

"Hmmm." Drake thought for a moment, then broke out into a comical smile. "Since he's a vampire like me, I think I'll name him after that dude from Twilight."

I laughed, which only goaded Drake on.

"Yup, Jacob, it is," he declared.

I didn't have the heart to tell him that Jacob was the werewolf. He seemed so proud of his namesake.

Merlin reappeared and gave us a solemn nod. "Luna understands. She just wants a promise that we'll be able to visit him sometimes."

"Dude!" Drake shouted. "Of course, you can. Come whenever you want. Any time. Seriously, any time."

"Then we should make haste before mama cat has the chance to change her mind," Fluffikins said.

Merlin and I returned to the cat family's nest to say goodbye.

"Bye, Jacob!" I called right before Fluffikins, Drake, and that precious little vampire kitty disappeared in a swirl of mist.

Luna blinked up at me. "Jacob? Since when is that his name?"

"Drake decided just now," I said, almost like an apology.

She sighed. "Then we should name the others, darling."

Merlin nodded. "Before we do, I have a request for Gracie."

"Sure. You can ask me anything. You know that." I settled onto the floor to bring us closer to eye level.

Merlin curled up on my lap, glancing up at me with huge honey brown eyes. "When I surrendered my magic, I freed you of the familiar contract. It was the only way to save you. But make no mistake, you were the best familiar a witch could ever ask for. I love you, and I'm so grateful that we found each other."

"I love you, too, Merlin," I said, admittedly tearing up now.

"Gracie, would you please help me find equally wonderful familiars to serve my children? I know it won't be easy, but I want them to have the best, just as I have had the b—"

"Merlin," I interrupted. "Choose me. I love your kittens as if they are my own. And I will serve them as I have served you. We'll all stay together as a family. That is, if it's okay with you."

Merlin and Luna exchanged glowing looks of love.

"We do not deserve you, dear," she cried. "But I am so happy we have you in our lives, anyway."

"Yes, Daisy, Rosie, and Honeysuckle are absolutely the luckiest kittens alive," Merlin said, bending down to lick his wife on the forehead.

Luna beamed up at him. "You mean...?"

"I know it was hard seeing our boy set off so young. We should give the girls the names you picked for them. Besides, they've grown on me."

The cats licked each other again, and I slowly backed out of the room to give the furry family its privacy.

I was part of that family, too, and I would devote myself to those three young ladies as long as I lived.

Sure, it wasn't the life I had planned for myself, but it's the one I'd made along the way.

And I was going to love every second of it.

My name is Gracie Springs, and I'm not a witch. But my life is pretty darned magical all the same.

You didn't think it was over, did you? Gracie will be back. As will Drake and Jake. Both in new series. Woohoo!

Make sure you're on my list so that you hear about all the new releases, monthly giveaways, and other cool stuff (including lots and lots of cat pics).

You can do that here:
MollyMysteries.com/subscribe

WHAT'S NEXT?

If you've never been to a magical cat wedding, then you are definitely missing out! But with so many supernatural creatures gathered in one small space, there's bound to be a kerfuffle or two. Luckily, Gracie Springs, resident human, wedding planner, and familiar extraordinaire, is on the case.

LUNA THE MAGICKLESS FLUFF is coming this fall as part of a special cozy mystery anthology. Subscribe to Molly's newsletter so you don't miss it!

You can do that here: MollyMysteries.com/subscribe

And until then... *(turn the page)*

MEET OCT-CAT

If you love Gracie and Merlin's magical antics, then you should meet the OG kitty detective, Octo-Cat. Read on for a special peek of KITTY PREVIEW, the first book in my Pet Whisperer P.I. series...

I was just your normal twenty-something with seven associate degrees and no idea what I wanted to do with my life. That is, until I died... Well, almost.

As if a near-death experience at the hands of an old coffeemaker wasn't embarrassing enough, I woke up to find I could talk to animals. Or rather one animal in particular.

His full name is Octavius Maxwell Ricardo

Edmund Frederick Fulton, but since that's way too long for anyone to remember, I've taken to calling him Octo-Cat. He talks so fast he can be difficult to understand, but seems to be telling me that his late owner didn't die of natural causes like everyone believes.

Well, now it looks like I no longer have a choice, apparently my life calling is to serve as Blueberry Bay's first ever pet whisperer P.I while maintaining my façade as a paralegal at the offices of Fulton, Thompson & Associates.

I just have one question: How did Dr. Dolittle make this gig look so easy?

KITTY CONFIDENTIAL is now available.

CLICK HERE to get your copy so that you can start reading this series today.

You can also turn the page to read the first chapter... Enjoy!

I woke up on the conference room floor. Funny, I couldn't remember passing out, yet there I was.

My heart womped a million miles an hour,

but most of my body had become fuzzy and tingly. I tried to move my arms, but they seemed content to lay splayed out at my sides. One by one, my senses started to come back online.

Pop!

Mrs. Fulton's shriek was the first thing I heard, then others in the room began to murmur amongst themselves. Some voices I recognized, but others were completely unfamiliar.

Bethany said, "It's probably time we threw that old thing out."

Mr. Fulton ignored her as he rushed toward me. "Angie... Angie..." His panicked voice grew closer until he'd arrived right at my side. "Are you okay?"

Meanwhile, Mr. Thompson mumbled something about liabilities and workman's compensation—exactly as anyone who knew him would expect him to do in such a situation.

I was still trying to remember what had happened when an unexpected weight pressed down onto my chest and made it quite difficult for me to breathe. The overpowering smell of tuna filled my nostrils, and the sudden intensity of it brought on a coughing fit.

A voice I'd never heard before hovered over me. "Well, how about that? This one had more than one life, after all. People, pssh. So fragile."

"Oh, she's breathing!" Diane shouted.

"Of course, she's breathing, honey," her husband responded with a note of relief in his previously panicked voice. "She's also coughing."

"And here I thought the car trip wouldn't be worth it," that same unfamiliar voice chimed in, pairing the words with an unkind chuckle. "That was, paws down, the best entertainment I've had all week."

Finally, my eyes flew open, and I found a gleaming amber gaze watching me from just a few inches away. Wait... Why was there a cat in the office, and why was it on me? I struggled to sit up, but my limbs were still too heavy to lift on my own.

"Oh, honey," that voice drawled again. "If you expect to keep walking, then you probably should have landed on your feet."

I let out a loud groan. I could feel the activity humming all around me, but the only thing I saw was the danged cat who was definitely intruding in my personal space right about then.

"What happened?" I asked before coughing again.

"I think the coffeemaker electrocuted you when you tried to plug it in," Diane revealed. Her shaky voice made it obvious she'd been crying. I felt so bad that my clumsiness put her through that.

"Oh, jeez. This one's even stupider than the first. I'm really looking forward to living with her while the rest of the family figures out where to dump me. Such a pity. They don't know greatness when it's staring them in the face."

I moaned and attempted to lift my head to get a better look around the room. "Who is that?" I demanded.

"It's me, Angie," Mrs. Fulton said, squeezing one of my hands in earnest. "You asked what happened, and I told you about the coffeemaker."

"No, the guy who just called both of us stupid." I wished I could sit up to see past this annoying cat, but he was the only thing that filled my vision in that moment. Of course, I had lots of questions about the coffeemaker and how such a tiny old appliance had managed to zap me unconscious, but the need to identify the unknown speaker weighed on me much more heavily.

A cruel snicker sounded nearby. "I called you stupid, because you are stupid. Honesty is the best policy, the truth will set you free, yada yada, and all that other nonsense you humans like to say."

If I hadn't known any better, I'd have sworn that strange, lilting voice was coming from the cat. Man, how hard had I hit my head when I fell?

The cat leaned in so close that his whiskers tickled my face. His unnervingly large eyes moved frantically from side to side as if stalking some kind of prey. Oh, how I hoped I wasn't that prey. I'd barely escaped the coffeemaker. If something sentient set out to hurt me today, I wouldn't even stand a chance.

"Did you... Did you really hear what I said?" the voice asked again, and again it really sounded like it was coming from the cat. Did he eat a tiny human or something? None of this made any sense.

"Yes, I hear you, and I think you're rather mean," I answered with a huff, giving the best attitude I could, considering my prone position.

"Angie, who are you talking to?" Diane asked with words that sounded unsure and just as worried as I felt myself.

"I'm not sure who it is, but he keeps insulting me." I closed my eyes tight, then slowly opened them again.

The cat seemed to smile, but not in a friendly way. Once again, I wondered if he considered me easy prey. Heck, I considered me easy prey, too.

"No one's insulting you," Mr. Fulton insisted. "We all just want to make sure you're okay."

The cat smiled again, bigger this time. "Ooh, ooh, me! I'm insulting you, you big, stupid bag of skin."

"He just called me a big, stupid bag of skin! Can you really not hear him?" I blinked half a dozen times, then pinched myself. Nothing seemed to change.

"Russo, I think maybe you should take the rest of the day off and a trip to the emergency room," Mr. Thompson commanded after clearing his throat loudly from somewhere near the door.

"Wow, you really can hear me," the voice said again. "By the way, hi, I'm Octavius Maxwell Ricardo Edmund Frederick Fulton, and I have some demands."

I was having a difficult time keeping track of all the threads of conversation. I knew the partners were worried about me and about themselves, but I still couldn't identify the mystery speaker or figure out what he wanted. "Octavius Maxwell... who?"

"Honey, are you talking about the cat?" Mrs. Fulton asked, picking the tabby off from my chest.

My straining lungs thanked her, and immediately I felt stronger.

In a cutesy baby voice, Diane held the cat up to her face and cooed, "Are you trying to help our Angie feel better? You're such a sweet fuzzy wuzzy."

The cat turned to me and narrowed his eyes into slits. "Heeeeelp meeeee."

Energized at last by my need to find out what the heck was going on, I managed to sit up and look around the room.

"Oh, good. Now that you can move again, Peters will take you to the hospital," Thompson decreed.

Bethany sighed but didn't argue the point.

"Wait!" The tabby cat trotted up to me the second Diane set him back on the floor. "What about my demands?"

I stared at him, dumbfounded. There was absolutely no way...

The cat flicked his tail and emitted a low growl from deep in his throat. "I know you can hear me, so how about doing the polite thing and keeping up your end of the conversation, huh?"

"What do you want?" I whispered, but still everyone in the office could see and hear the crazy lady talking to the cat she'd just met.

"My owner was murdered, and I need you to help me prove it. Also, of equal importance, I haven't been fed in hours. Maybe years." His ears fell back against his head and his eyes widened, making me feel inexplicably fond of him despite his bad attitude.

Then the first part of what he said hit me, and I gasped. "Murdered?"

Bethany tittered nervously and grabbed me by the arm. "Okay, let's get you to the hospital. Hallucinations are not a good sign."

"But..." I began to argue. That argument fell away when I realized I had no sane or valid reason to resist.

"Murdered!" the cat shouted after me dramatically. "She was offed before her time, and now that I know you can hear me, you're going to help me get her the justice she deserves. It's the least I can do to thank her for all the years she spent feeding me and arranging my pillows just as I like them. Also, did you hear the part about me needing to be fed?"

KITTY CONFIDENTIAL is now available.

CLICK HERE to get your copy so that you can start reading this series today.

MORE MOLLY

ABOUT MOLLY FITZ

While USA Today bestselling author Molly Fitz can't technically talk to animals, she and her doggie best friend, Sky Princess, have deep and very animated conversations as they navigate their days. Add to that, five more dogs, a snarky feline, comedian husband, and diva daughter, and you can pretty much imagine how life looks at the Casa de Fitz.

Molly lives in a house on a high hill in the Michigan woods and occasionally ventures out for good food, great coffee, or to meet new animal friends.

Writing her quirky, cozy animal mysteries

is pretty much a dream come true, but sometimes she also goes by the names Melissa Storm and Mila Riggs and writes a very different kind of story.

Learn more, grab the free app, or sign up for her newsletter at **www. MollyMysteries.com**!

PET WHISPERER P.I.

Angie Russo just partnered up with Blueberry Bay's first ever talking cat detective. Along with his ragtag gang of human and animal helpers, Octo-Cat is determined to save the day... so long as it doesn't interfere with his schedule. Start with book 1, *Kitty Confidential.*

PARANORMAL TEMP AGENCY

Tawny Bigford's simple life takes a turn for the magical when she stumbles upon her landlady's murder and is recruited by a talking black cat named Fluffikins to take over the deceased's role as the official Town Witch for Beech Grove, Georgia. Start with book 1, **Witch for Hire.**

MERLIN THE MAGICAL FLUFF

Gracie Springs is not a witch... but her cat is. Now she must help to keep his secret or risk spending the rest of her life in some magical prison. Too bad trouble seems to find them at every turn! Start with book 1, **Merlin the Magical Fluff.**

THE MEOWING MEDIUM

Mags McAllister lives a simple life making candles for tourists in historic Larkhaven, Georgia. But when a cat with mismatched eyes enters her life, she finds herself with the ability to see into the realm of spirits... Now the ghosts of people long dead have started coming to her for help solving their cold cases. Start with book 1, **Secrets of the Specter.**

THE PAINT-SLINGING SLEUTH

Following a freak electrical storm, Lisa Lewis's vibrant paintings of fairytale creatures have started coming to life. Unfortunately, only she can see and communicate with them. And when her mentor turns up dead, this aspiring artist must turn amateur sleuth to clear her name and save the day with only these "pigments" of her imagination to help her. Start with book 1, **My Colorful Conundrum.**

SPECIAL COLLECTIONS

Pet Whisperer P.I. Books 1-3
Pet Whisperer P.I. Books 4-6
Pet Whisperer P.I. Books 7-9
Pet Whisperer P.I. Books 10-12

CONNECT WITH MOLLY

You can download my free app here:
mollymysteries.com/app

Or sign up for my newsletter and get a special digital prize pack for joining, including an exclusive story, Meowy Christmas Mayhem, fun quiz, and lots of cat pictures!
mollymysteries.com/subscribe

Have you ever wanted to talk to animals? You can chat with Octo-Cat and help him solve an exclusive online mystery here:

mollymysteries.com/chat

Or maybe you'd like to chat with other animal-loving readers as well as to learn about new books and giveaways as soon as they happen! Come join Molly's VIP reader group on Facebook.

mollymysteries.com/group

MORE BOOKS LIKE THIS

Welcome to Whiskered Mysteries, where each and every one of our charming cozies comes with a furry sidekick... or several! Around here, you'll find we're all about crafting the ultimate reading experience. Whether that means laugh-out-loud antics, jaw-dropping magical exploits, or whimsical journeys through small seaside towns, you decide.

So go on and settle into your favorite comfy chair and grab one of our *paw*some cozy mysteries to kick off your next great reading adventure!

Visit our website to browse our books and
meet our authors, to jump into our
discussion group, or to join our newsletter.
See you there!

www.WhiskeredMysteries.com

WHISKMYS (WĬSK′MƏS)

DEFINITION : a state of fiction-induced euphoria that commonly occurs in those who read books published by the small press, Whiskered Mysteries.

USAGE: Every day is Whiskmys when you have great books to read!

LEARN MORE AT
WWW.WHISKMYS.COM

Made in the USA
Monee, IL
29 June 2021